# CASCADING PETALS

# JANE C. BRADY

Cover Designer: Victoria Cooper Art
Facebook: www.facebook.com/VictoriaCooperArt

Editing: Editing4Indies
Website: www.editing4indies.com

Formatter: Champagne Book Design

Interior Illustration by Autumn C.

ISBN: 978-1-7750676-3-4

# DEDICATION

For my daughter, your strength and courage are an inspiration. May you always stay true to yourself and continue to pave your own path in life.

For all the children, out there who have struggled to survive in the school world. Please know you are not alone and you are worthy of respect and love as much as the next person.

*Illustration by Autumn C.*

# CHAPTER ONE

*Jewel*

S enior year held no promises for improvement. Someone had once told me that high school would be better than all the years before it. So far, that's not been the case. I dared to hope my senior year would finally make up for all the rest.

The anxiety of a new school year picked at me as I sat at the beige granite kitchen island, scarfing my breakfast down. Soon, I'd wander upstairs to search through my endless closet of clothes and come up with the same conclusion. Nothing I chose would make me feel everything about me wasn't all wrong.

When I looked in the mirror, I saw a blue-eyed blonde peering back at me. Was I pretty? Sure. But I saw what all the other kids saw. The loser… the girl who wasn't cool enough or good enough to belong.

Friends? What were those? I wanted one person to give

me a chance, but I'd never had any. Was that so much to ask? Being friendless had been my story for as long as I could recall.

"Earth to Jewel." My older brother's voice cut through my thoughts as he plopped down beside me.

"Don't start." I glared at Miles, anxiety pulling at me.

He raised a hand in surrender. "Okay, chill. No need to get riled up."

I huffed a sigh. "I'm sorry."

Miles shrugged off my reply and dived into his bowl of Cheerios. At two years older than I was, I wouldn't say we were close, but I knew he loved me. Miles was the quiet type of guy. Girls thought he was smoking hot—our mother's Italian heritage giving him dark hair and dark eyes—but he'd yet to let one catch his attention. Goal oriented, Miles had worked since he was fifteen, purchasing the shiny black Silverado out in the driveway with straight cash. He was that kind of guy. I admired and looked up to him. On the nights when he found me crying in my room over something that happened at school, he would sit with me and offer me comfort. He'd joke around and tell me only he had permission to pick on me, often securing a laugh from me.

I recalled a time in junior high when a group of boys came up to me at the bus stop. I dropped my eyes as soon as I saw them because I was a favorite target of theirs.

My body curled inward as they mocked me.

On this day, Miles happened to be in the right place at the right time and walked up. Miles had taken the boy by the arm and given him a rough shake. Things like that made him who he was in my eyes.

"Morning, kiddos," Mom's cheerful voice pierced my thoughts.

"Morning," Miles and I replied in unison.

She started the coffeemaker before turning to us. Her dark brown bedhead stood up on end, and squinting through sleepy eyes, she smiled at us.

"Well, the last year of high school for you, baby girl, and the beginning of university for you, bud," she said with a chuckle, tucking the belt of her cream-colored fleece robe snugly around her.

"School is the pits," I grumbled.

"Or I could live with you forever and bypass school altogether," Miles said with a smirk at Mom.

Maybe it was because he was her firstborn, but my mom had a soft place in her heart just for him. Always the smart one, Miles was well aware of this and sometimes used it to his advantage. He'd bat his chocolate-brown puppy dog eyes at her, and Mom seemed to melt under his spell.

"You can live with me as long as you need to, but you'll still be a productive citizen in society." She scrunched her eyebrows and laughed. "But nice try."

I smiled at their carefree banter as Mom brushed stray crumbs off the countertop with her hand.

"Morning, family," Dad said, humming as he sauntered into the chef's kitchen he designed for Mom. He was dressed in a pinstripe charcoal suit. Beneath the collar of his crisp white dress shirt hung a deep purple tie, not yet tied. His blond locks were tapered short on the sides while the top was left longer and combed back. He resembled one of those middle-aged men you saw in cologne ads.

He wrapped my mom in his arms for a quick kiss and a squeeze. Then he rounded the counter to place a kiss on top of my head before giving me an encouraging hug, as if to say,

"You've got this." He ruffled my brother's neatly gelled back hair.

"Dad!" Miles said with a groan, but a grin curved his mouth.

Dad grabbed a stool at the island, and Mom placed a piping-hot cup of coffee in front of him.

I loved how my parents loved each other. Don't get me wrong—they could be as annoying as any other parents, but overall, they were great. They were there for us, unwavering in their love and support.

"What do you guys say to a trip to New Orleans over Christmas break?" Mom smiled, a glimmer of excitement in her hazel eyes.

"I'm in," Dad said without hesitation.

As a lawyer at our family firm, my dad worked long, grueling hours. Family vacations were his escape.

"Good, because we're going." Mom grinned.

I glanced at the time on my smartphone. "Well, I need to go get ready, so I will see you guys later," I said, hopping down from the nail-studded ivory leather barstool.

The sun was sneaking through the cream silk curtains in my bedroom, its rays painting a long, narrow window on my dark hardwood floor. I ambled to the window and pulled aside the curtains, glancing out over our neighborhood. Our house sat tucked back from the street, and the broad expanse of lawn between the neighboring homes provided a sense of privacy. A circular driveway surrounded the front of our two-story sandstone concrete house. Windows stretching on forever mirrored the broad red maples lining our property.

Shuffling to my double-door walk-in closet, I grasped the glass doorknob and flicked on the light. The ivory-colored chandelier's faceted crystal pendants reflected the light, blinding my early morning eyes. The vaulted ceiling made the closet feel like a room of its own. Shoes and purses in various styles and colors were neatly stored individually to showcase them. In the center of the back wall, a large window provided additional light within the soft metallic gray walls. Ceiling-to-floor glass doors displayed rows of white shelving with color-coordinated clothing. In the center sat an ivory leather chaise with an oversized ruffled pale pink pillow placed on it. A smaller silver pillow with the word "love" embroidered on it sat in the center of the chaise.

I stood back and stared at my choices, but nothing jumped out at me. Summer was still making its presence known, forcasting a smoldering twenty-eight degrees Celsius in Toronto today. I first tried a knee-length pale yellow sundress with tiny pink flowers. The rayon dress nipped in at the waist, then flowed into jagged layers. The adorable criss-cross of ties exposed my back, which I embraced as a good feature. Summer days lying by the pool drinking lemonade had given me a sun-kissed glow. Looking in the floor-length mirror, I scrutinized myself from every angle.

"Blah," I grumbled.

The dress made me feel wide through the hips. I tugged down the sides, trying to make it a few inches longer to cover the bruise on my right leg from a tumble during my horse-riding class. With a sigh, I whipped it over my head and placed it back on the hanger. Next choice was a pair of white jean shorts. I slid into them and gave my butt a glance in the mirror. I liked my curves, but some days—like today—I viewed myself as fat. Logically, at five foot two and one hundred and ten pounds, I knew I wasn't, but after years of my peers having nothing better to do than pick on me, I'd developed a negative opinion of my appearance. Once, a disparaging girl said I was fat, and I shouldn't be seen eating in public. Can you believe that? Guys could eat in public, and it was cool, but girls were supposed to hide in shame. Even though I knew this remark was insane, it stayed in my head, starting years of refusing to eat lunch at school.

Looked like jeans and a tank was what it was going to be. I grabbed a pair of the medium-wash jeans Mom had purchased for me for back to school. I slid them on and zipped them up. I liked how they tucked in all my imperfections and how the edginess of the rips trailed down my legs.

"Knock, knock."

I clutched a white ribbed tank from the shelf and poked my head out the closet door. "Hey, Mom, what's up?"

"I'm going to get your sister up and get myself ready for the office. I wanted to wish you a good day in case you leave before I see you again." She smiled softly. Mom ran the accounting department at the firm, but no matter how busy she was, she always put us kids first. I counted on her more than I cared to admit. She was my strength when my supply was depleted.

"Thanks, Mom," I replied. "Maybe this will be my year." I glanced at her for encouragement.

"I hope so, Jewel." She willed an encouraging smile, but her eyes reflected the pain we had both struggled with throughout my school years.

I knew my life of ill treatment had affected her. She was one of those moms who became a mama bear when you messed with her cubs. She hated conflict as much as the next person, but when it came to her children, she'd go toe to toe with any parent, teacher, or anyone else threatening us. Don't get me wrong—she didn't run to my defense all the time, but when things were beyond my ability to fix, she stepped in.

"Remember, they're the ones with the issues, not you. They're the ones hurting inside, and you just happen to be the one they spew it out on. It's not right, but try not to let it hurt you. Like I always say, 'You're beautiful and strong.' Hold your chin up and don't take any of their trash-talk. You've got this, Jewel," she said with determination.

I smiled at her and her effort to instill hope in me. God bless her for trying, but it didn't take away the heaviness deep in my stomach or the nausea threatening to overtake me.

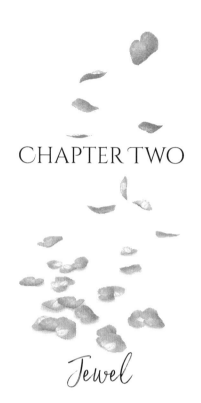

# CHAPTER TWO

*Jewel*

Y ork Mills High School was like a billboard of gray brick with a modern contemporary appeal. Glass structured wings jutted out, expanding across the school property. Concrete sidewalks led to the wide stairs extending up to the front entrance. A Canadian flag flapped and cracked in the wind at the top of a flagpole.

In the student parking zone, I parked my white 2012 Honda Civic. My parents purchased the car for my sixteenth birthday. Gathering my khaki green backpack from the back seat, I slung the straps over my shoulder. The weight of the binders and supplies for the new year dug into my shoulder.

Cheers to wishing this year would be the start of something new. I plighted a hope.

Only one year left.

I exhaled a long breath before setting my feet in motion to the nightmare that's been my school life. Bullying had defined my life since that one day in kindergarten.

*I headed out for recess, eager to find the two girls I thought were my friends. They were waiting for me at the corner of the school, but the looks on their faces confused me.*

*"We've decided we don't want to be friends with you anymore," one girl said.*

*"But why?" I asked.*

*"Because we don't like you."*

*I started to cry. "What did I do?"*

*She pushed me backward. "I said we don't like you."*

*"Yeah," the other one piped in and gave me another shove, sending me toppling down the snow hill.*

*"Get her," the second girl squealed.*

*The first one proceeded to sit on me and jammed my face into the ground. My front teeth clanked against a hunk of ice. I screamed as hot blood ran over my teeth and stained the snow a cherry red. The nerve damage shading my two front teeth gray lasted until my baby teeth fell out.*

In the younger years, I was targeted for being meek, but as I got older, it became something entirely different. For the past few years, my teachers had told my mom it was because I was a triple threat. Triple threat meaning I was pretty, talented, and the boys liked me. I personally didn't know why, but Mom stuck to the same theory.

I cut across the freshly trimmed grass. Buses of out of town students unloaded in the bus zone. Parents in their luxury cars pulled to the front curb to drop off their sophomore kids. The air resonated with the muttering of students, and the pitch of their jubilant voices increased as students met up with their friends. Guys exchanged enthusiastic fist pumps and 'Hey, dude' and 'What's up man.' Girls air-kissed and squealed in delight. With their heads huddled together, they floated off to catch up on their grand summer adventures.

I surveyed them with a forlorn envy. What would it be like to have someone welcome me on my first day? Or to have someone waiting on my arrival?

Then I saw him—the new guy.

He walked with an electrifying confidence, owning the space around him. His broad shoulders nudged through the herds of students. I didn't miss the girls who paused midstep as their jaws unhinged, their eyes resembling binoculars as they soaked in the new eye candy.

A few weeks back, I had the pleasure of meeting the honey-brown eyed, six-foot Kaiden Carter. I had a quick stop at the coffee shop by my parents' office to thank for that.

His voice snapped me back to the present moment.

"Hello, again." His dimples appeared with his smile.

"Hello," I returned with a leery smile.

"Jewel, isn't it?" he asked, adjusting the binders in his arms.

"Yes, that's right."

"Well, here goes nothing, hey?" He waved a hand at our surroundings.

"Yup," I replied, my eyes glued straight ahead.

He softly chuckled. "I may have to label you the one-word wonder as you don't seem to talk much." He glanced sideways at me as we walked.

"I do. But I…never mind." I peered down at my red Converse.

"Maybe you can introduce me to some other students. Kind of rough starting at a new school and feeling alone."

"Tell me about it," I mumbled under my breath.

"What did you say?" He bent his head down to hear, a light breeze blowing through his dark waves.

"I wish I could help you fit in, but I struggle with it myself."

"How so?" He knitted his brow.

"Unfortunately, it is the sad truth. Friends aren't my forte. For some reason, I have ended up a loner. Girls formed their cliques and didn't have room for me, and guys have proved to be a waste of time."

"You seem likable enough to me," he said, peering at me with piqued curiosity.

I shot him a glance and shrugged my shoulders. "It's how it is with me."

"Surely, you've had a good friend at one time or another?"

"No. Girls are hard. They are friends with you one day and gone the next. It's how it is in the girl world," I said. "You sure have a lot of questions for a five-minute acquaintance." A buoyant laugh came from me as I paused to read him.

He stopped and turned to look at me. "What? The other day at the coffee shop didn't count?" He grinned down on me, pinching his dimples tighter.

I ran my eyes over his simple white t-shirt paired with jeans and a brown leather jacket. I couldn't deny he was attractive. I gave my head a shake and focused back on him. "Look, Kyle—"

"It's Kaiden, actually. But you can call me Kai." He flashed me a pearly white grin.

The ring of the bell startled me, and I jumped. "I've got to get to class. I'll see you around." I twirled on my heels and hastened my pace. A new page in the history of Jewel Hart had been written with my sudden itch to get to class.

## *Kaiden*

The sway of her hips as she hurried away captivated my focus. She'd invaded my mind since the day I first saw her at the coffee shop. When the aftertaste of her overly sweet latte rebelled against my taste buds. That Wednesday afternoon marked the third anniversary of my dad's death. My mom had struggled to function after his death and was having one of her crippling dark days. The shadows of depression engulfed her, and in her drug-induced irritation, she lashed out. She didn't mean to, but she often directed her pain at me. I mulled over the disease that took my dad and the mental illness robbing me of my mom, who'd once been a woman of adventure, positivity, and perseverance. My protectiveness of her over the years enabled her to spend her days hidden away in her room. I learned to adapt to the parental role of caring for her and hid our grave situation from outsiders. But when we lost everything, my grandparents had to step in and moved us to live with them here in York Mills. With our recent move, I noticed her spells of depression weren't quite so often. A glimmer of the mother of my past started to emerge. My grandparents could offer her the extra support she needed, and they convinced her to attend a local support group. She still had her days, but the future held a glint of hope.

I stood in the crowded coffee shop, lost in my sorrows and constant worry about my mom. Blotting out the existence of everything around me, I waited for my order. At the pickup order area, the barista called out an order. Eager to be on my way, I grabbed the drink she set on the counter in front of me. I inhaled one sip of the hot, sugary syrup, and as it ran over my tongue, I coughed in alarm but managed to refrain from spitting it out. I looked at the black marker handwriting scrawled on the side of the cup. *Jewel.* I turned to see whose sugar high I'd stolen, and my eyes settled on the striking tawny-haired five-foot-nothing watching me fiercely as I poached her liquid gold. Her intense close-set aquamarine blue eyes clutched my gaze.

"My mistake. Are you Jewel?"

"Yes."

"My apologies. Let me order you another," I said as I read the label: *Caramel Macchiato.* I promptly got back in the dreadfully long line and purchased a new one. I grabbed my lukewarm Americano and swerved to speak to her. "Are you from around here?"

"Yes."

"Good to know. Do you attend York Mills High School?" I went on to inquire.

"Yes." Her brow furrowed, and her gazed probed mine.

"I'm Kaiden Carter. I recently moved here, so maybe I'll see you around?"

"Sure."

"Jewel, hun, here is a fresh latte," said the tan-from-a-bottle lady behind the counter as she handed her, her beverage. She thanked the lady and promptly left without a glimpse in my direction.

I stared at her until she disappeared around the side of the building.

The barista's voice cut through my thoughts as she said, "Her name is Jewel Hart." She concreted a smile on her wrong-shade-of-pink lipstick lips.

Even though the middle-aged woman had gotten her

appearance all wrong, her mannerisms exuded a friendly warmness. She nudged her box-dyed ash blonde head toward the building next door. She went on to inform me the lovely creature who just departed worked across the street at the law firm in the summer for her parents. I exited the coffee shop and glanced up at the multiple story glass building. It displayed a massive sign which read Hart and D'amico Law Firm in bold, scripted letters.

Now, as I watched her disappear into the mob of buzzing students, I was yet again left captivated by the empty space she had inhabited. Something was normal and secure about her. I would guess from our short exchanges that life had scarred her soul, causing the guarded way she held her body and the flicker of distrust that coated her eyes and tugged at her full mouth.

I pushed through the heavy metal, glass-paned doors into the last of the long list of schools I had attended in recent years. I weaved through the corridor of swarming students to my first class. When entering the room, a bald man standing well below average in height greeted me.

"Welcome to chemistry class. The students call me Mr. B," he said with a smile stretched across his face, tweaking the laugh lines engraved in the corners of his green eyes.

Taking an instant liking to him, I grinned down at him. "Thanks."

I sprinted to the back of the classroom and glided into an open seat. The bell signaled the beginning of class, and as Mr. B started to speak, an unusual hush fell over the room. I glanced around at my classmates to find their eyes pinned on him. He clearly earned their respect as a teacher, and I settled in for the next eighty minutes.

# CHAPTER THREE

*Jewel*

Ticktock, ticktock. I stared at the oversized clock on the wall at the front of my English classroom. The sound of Mrs. Barker's monotone voice as she recited Shakespeare's *Hamlet* dulled my senses. The stuffiness of the classroom made my eyelids droop. I muffled a yawn behind my copy of *Hamlet*.

Mrs. Barker earned herself a reputation for having her favorites or pet student per se. The word around school was she picked on students who didn't fall into her category of chosen ones. When I spotted her name on my list of classes, my nerves gnawed. I was determined to keep my head down and avoid her snare.

The clicking of her orange fluorescent heels on the taupe-speckled vinyl tiles grated at me. Her fiery-red hair hung long and heavy like a cheap wig. The denim blue sleeveless blouse she wore revealed the three-quarter-length sleeve tattoo covering her right arm. She calculatedly outlined and arched her eyes in black eyeliner to achieve an overdramatic extended cat-eye appearance.

My attention span drifted involuntary to the disinterested students around me and gridlocked on Lexi Clark. As expected, she sat close to the front of the class. Above all the rest, she was one of Mrs. Barker's *chosen ones*. I'd seen them walking the halls last year laughing and carrying on like they were besties. Lexi didn't like her any more than the next student; she simply tolerated Mrs. Barker because it earned her favoritism. I'd known Lexi since junior high, and for a time, we actually were friends. Until she turned on me … and I'd become her target ever since.

After all these years, I still couldn't wrap my brain around why I had become a walking bull's-eye for people to unload their internal issues on. Maybe my lack of self-esteem had aided in the nastiness they ejected on me. Or maybe it was their lack of control over their own lives and their own inner self-hate. In their desperation to find a release, I happened to be the lucky winner. This unjust world became my reality.

Throughout my freshman year, I had tried to fit in, and even lowered my standards once or twice to belong in their clique. Until I began to resent myself and them for who I'd become. The gatekeeper of self-worth continued to enforce her mom views of selling my soul to fit in. Mom's continued guidance on demanding respect helped me believe in my self-worth, and my wayward ways halted. I began to require more of myself and the ones around me. It didn't help me make friends, nor did it make me like myself any more, but it did give me something to grasp onto.

On the outside looking in, I appeared to have it all. A

loving family and parents who were checked in and present in our lives. They traveled the world with us, and I had all the luxuries a teenager could want. But I didn't have the one thing I yearned, which was to belong and be accepted. I struggled within myself to figure out why because becoming friends with a girl or group of girls would eventually lead to me being excluded and left behind.

After years of ill-treatment and bullying, I formed a shell of defense. Girls who ran in cliques, in my experience, were cruel and catty, often showing no mercy and going straight for the jugular. If they weren't attacking me physically, they would try to go after my family. Anything to raise them up and leave me scratching at the ground looking for the will to go on.

"Miss Hart, is it?"

My heart seized.

I smelled her sickly floral perfume, which had my stomach churning all morning. Her shadow hovered over my desk. Peeking up, I found her scowling down at me.

"Yes, that's correct." I managed to forge a faint smile.

"I expect you to be focused and attentive in my class. I have no time for dreamers. Got it?" she said with an arctic stare.

"Yes."

Good job, Jewel. You couldn't fly under the radar.

The sharp slap of her hand on my desk jarred my nerves, and I jerked back. My reaction caused a satisfied smirk on her thin, red-painted lips.

"Maybe now, I can get back to teaching the students who want to be here." She straightened her plump figure. Circling me one time, she made sure to exude her authority, then she swayed to the front of the class, pausing briefly at Lexi's desk. Mrs. Barker smiled a nauseating, worshiping smile upon her. "I absolutely adore that color on you, Lexi."

Lexi showered her with an Academy award-winning fake smile. "Thanks, Mrs. Barker. My mom got this shirt for my birthday." She admired herself in her too-revealing spaghetti-strap teal top.

Lexi Clark. Let me tell you a little about her. She aimed to rule the school these past two years. Mean was her middle name, and she had successfully accomplished the mean girl mentality. Yet the underlying cause of her meanness was her broken home life. Abandoned by her dad, she was the definition of a girl with daddy issues. Because of this, I'd allowed my heart to feel a bit of compassion for her. She portrayed herself to be superior, exuding a high level of confidence, but I knew this to be her coping mechanism. I'd taken the brunt of her personal hatred for years, and in some twisted way, it made her feel better. How someone could feel better after inflicting pain on others, I couldn't quite understand.

Her lowest of low attack on my self-esteem was in grade ten in the girls' changing room before gym. *I lifted the sweater I was wearing over my head and was struggling to get out of it when someone's hand went to the clasp of my bra strap. I jerked to move away as the clasp released. My breasts fell out and were exposed to the other girls in the changing room. In horror, I untangled myself from the sweater and covered myself. Tears scalded my eyes as Lexi's laughter seared my ears.*

*"So you don't stuff it?" She pointed at my breasts. "Guess we were wrong, Jess. She does have some."*

*"It appears so. Still doesn't change the fact she needs make-up to cover up the ugly mug of hers."*

*I wanted to say something, but I was so horrified I couldn't move.* No words could describe the humiliation I felt when that memory popped into my head.

Mrs. Barker's voice drew me back. "Well, it suits you," she said with a light touch to Lexi's shoulder before spinning to address the class. "Class, I would like to finish up our lesson on *Hamlet* by the end of the week. I will be expecting an essay on my desk by Monday."

A chorus of groans resonated through the class at the logical requirement to do homework. The chime of the end of second-period was a welcoming relief. I gathered my books and made a beeline for the door.

The cafeteria had been hijacked by students. Their murmuring voices were like buzzing vultures scouring for their next meal. I stepped in line and secured a plastic orange tray. In front of me, an overweight girl with chestnut, shoulder-length tight curls spoke in hushed tones to her pretty, willowy Jamaican friend. They were considered part of the bookworm club. Sensing my gaze, their conversation hushed. I smiled an inviting smile at them. They graced me with an unwieldy half-smile before turning back to continue their exchange on the anticipation of the release of a book. At least these stereotyped bookworms had each other.

A shove clipped me from behind as Chad Palmer and Eric Jackson from the swim team lurched into line behind me. Chad was Lexi's current boyfriend. These guys were your typical jocks. Endless parties on the weekends. They left a trail of pathetic drooling girls in their fading footmarks. From there, they differed altogether. Chad had it all—wealth, popularity, the girls, the hot car. He was tall, rugged, and a pretty boy with his short blond waves and piercing, cobalt blue eyes. Like Lexi, he put the 'S' in selfish and added a bold capital at the beginning. He capped the egotistical category.

Eric ended up on the complete opposite end of the spectrum. His dad ran off with his mom's best friend, leaving his mom to care for him and his younger brother. Summer of grade nine and ten, he earned extra cash by doing lawn maintenance for my parents.

"Oh, sorry about that, Jewel," Eric said, using his free hand to steady me. His brandy brown eyes emitted kindness. Though we'd never become friends, he was always polite and respectful to me. Even if I frowned on him for hanging with the likes of Chad Palmer. Eric was amiable, and I considered him to be one of the good ones.

Chad's appreciative eyes pored over me. My skin crawled at his boorish intent.

"Sweet curves, baby," he said followed by a wet whistle. He reached out and brazenly stroked my collarbone with the back of his hand before he started to trail down my cleavage.

"Stop," I sputtered, staggering back out of his reach.

Mortified, I tugged my cardigan snugly around myself. Heat embodied my cheeks at his insinuations.

"What the hell, Chad?" Eric aligned a critical glare at him.

Chad scoffed. "What? You want first dibs on her dude or what?"

"Back off her. She isn't that kind of girl." Eric said, squaring his shoulders as his body weight shifted.

"Please, Jackson, don't dictate to me what I should and shouldn't do." Angry and embarrassed at being called out for his presumptuous ways, his face reddened.

"Relax, Chad," Eric stated his own discontent.

"Excuse me, can I help you?" I heard the annoyed cafeteria lady behind the counter shout at me.

Swiveling to her, I sputtered out my order. Swiftly, I retrieved a white milk and a banana and deposited them on my shaking tray. In my desire to flee, I thrust my money at her and told her to keep the change. I found an empty table in the middle of the room.

Humiliation entombed me, and acid tears threatened to shed from my eyes. Eric was right; I wasn't one of those girls. For Chad to even think I was open to the vulgarness I'd seen guys like him openly imply on girls without any repercussions was revolting.

I poked at the tossed salad on my tray. Picking up the packet of ranch dressing, I drowned my salad in it along with my sorrows. Anger pillaged me at the crap I continued to endure. I was so sick of this place. University couldn't come fast enough.

During my ninth grade year, my mom homeschooled me in hopes of taking me away from the toxicity school had caused in my life. Selflessly, she added my schooling on top of her excruciating schedule. During that year, I learned more about myself, and an inner strength grew in me. My parents signed me up for therapy with a local counselor and riding lessons at a local ranch as another form of therapy. At the ranch, I found a new love, and it became my escape from the loneliness. I excelled at western riding. I even volunteered on Mondays in hopes of brightening my resume for pursuing my dreams of a career as a vet. Thus beginning my ongoing road to self-discovery.

"Do you mind if I sit?" His velvety voice pummeled my moment of reflecting.

I glance up into Kaiden's enticing and welcoming eyes. Like pools of hot fudge, trickling down a sundae on a summer day, they warmed my depleted heart.

"I was actually saving these empty seats for all my friends who are going to show up, never." I gestured to the human-less blue plastic chairs.

"Well, when they arrive, I'll move out. How about that?" he engaged.

I laughed. "Sounds like a plan. The chairs are yours then."

Sitting, he unwrapped his Italian sub, and without hesitation, he took a big bite and after finishing his mouth full, he asked, "A girl like you should be surrounded by friends. What's the deal?"

"Your guess is as good as mine. It's been this way all my life."

He shuffled in his seat, and I began to doubt myself. "Well, it's quite simple, then isn't it?" he asserted nonchalantly.

My eyebrows knitted together in confusion. "I don't believe I follow you." He appeared to be a straight shooter, and I was drawn to this.

"You threaten them. You are beautiful, charming, and seem to be the kind of girl a guy can be himself around. I don't know much about you, but this is my first take on the situation," he said, resting his gaze on me.

A slew of exotic butterflies tumbled around in my chest, and I broke our gaze. Surprisingly, I didn't analyze his words for a double meaning.

"Whatever it may be, it does grow exhausting after a while," I said grimly. "Enough about that. What about you? Where do you come from?"

"Well, Jewel Hart, you will have to grace me with a first date if you wish to know more." His mouth curved in merriment.

Students started filtering out of the cafeteria to get to class. Kaiden stood, gathered his tray, and shot me a wink as he sauntered off.

He knew my last name. Had he asked about me? I watched him as he walked to the counter and handed his tray to the volunteer acne-covered grade-eleven student. His polite 'thank you' grasped my ears, and the wide smile he offered her grabbed at my heart. Her face flushed a scarlet red, and she clumsily returned his smile. It was my turn to sit back with a gaping mouth. Maybe Kaiden Carter was a guy of substance? What were the chances?

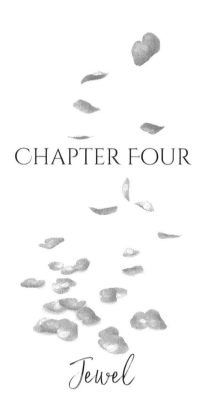

# CHAPTER FOUR

*Jewel*

T he infernal shrill of the last block bell sounded, announcing the end of the first day of my senior year. Like rabid cavemen, the student body clawed through the front doors, spilling into the fresh sun-soaked air.

One day down, one hundred and eighty-four to go, I grieved, scurrying to my car. Placing my backpack on the roof, I dug through my purse for my keys. As I shuffled around in the bottomless black pit, my water bottle slipped from the crook of my armpit.

Grumbling to myself, I bent to retrieve it. As if magnetically forced, the ground summoned the bottle, and it rolled stopping exactly in the center of the car.

You've got to be kidding me.

I placed my purse on the roof before dropping to my knees. Still not low enough, I laid flat on my stomach. Pressing my cheek against the hot sandpaper asphalt, I extended my fingertips as far as they could reach. The tip of my middle finger flicked the bottle, and it began to roll toward me until I could grasp it.

Gotcha!

The victory was short lived when I noticed three sets of feet paused on the other side of my car. My heart catapulted into the depths of my stomach as her orotund voice clipped my ears.

"I'm glad you finally found where you belong, Hart." Lexi's condescending remark irked the irritation started by the run away water bottle. I pinched my eyes shut. My lashes brushed the pavement as I gathered my wits.

Here we go. Why couldn't I claim one year without this bull crap?

Planting my palms on the ground, I pushed myself up to my knees. Before jumping up to face the green-eyed python and her nest of slithering babies. Who peered down at me, hissing their slithering tongues.

Lexi smirked as our eyes connected. She postured her curvy, almost plump frame as she snorted at me with disgust. Amy and Jess, her back scratchers, stood looking on. I glared at the girls, knowing their intent was to belittle me. Lexi tilted her brunette ponytailed head as she assessed me. Her fingers clutched the high-end designer bag her mom purchased for her as a beginning of the year present. How did I know this? She made sure to inform everyone as she had glided into first period class.

My internal temperature peaking. "What do you want, Lexi?"

"Oh, I want nothing from you," she mocked. Extravagantly placing a hand on her chest at the audacity of my insinuation.

Jess tossed her straight bleached blond hair over her shoulder as she trotted around my car. "Nice wheels." She ran her hot pink nails over the hood. "Did they have a special at the junkyard?"

My blood coiled. I wanted to smack the upturned nose right off her snickering face. The auburn-haired one, Amy, stood in the shadows of the girls with her gaze downturned. I eyed her briefly. Sensing my gaze, she looked up at me, her wavering green eyes pleading her apologies. In all honesty, she was the prettiest of the three. But she had allowed herself to become the bottom of the food chain of the group.

"Unlike your parents, Jessica, my parents don't give me everything in life. We have to work for the extras we want. People call it making yourself accountable. You should try it sometime. It may be a better look for you." I served an intentional dig.

"Oh, I see we hit a nerve." Lexi's eyes grew bright. She circled me like a hyena licking its lips as it regarded its prey. My insides curled as anxiety rose.

"Jewel, there you are." His melodic voice sounded.

We all turned, transfixing our sights on Kaiden. As he jogged toward us, he had his jacket slung over his shoulder, revealing his toned arms.

I breathed my relief at his appearance.

"Hi, Kaiden," I greeted him, feigning a casualty between us.

I glanced at the awestruck threesome. They gazed at Kaiden with glossy eyes, brimming with admiration.

He strolled up to me and dangled his arm around my shoulder, pulling me into his side. His chest was firm and defined beneath his white t-shirt. I sucked in a breath and goose bumps covered my entire body.

"I wanted to see if we're still on for a game of catch after school." He gazed dreamily at me.

Never quick on the draw, I stumbled a reply. "Umm, yes. Yes, we are," I managed to say.

"Good." He charmed me and the girls with a gleaming smile.

He turned to the girls. "So … what are you all chatting about?" His smile faded as he inspected them.

"We were … we …" Lexi stuttered as she glanced from him to me with an open mouth.

I knew her enough to know she was speculating how I managed to snag Kaiden before she could. She shook her Moroccan oiled dark locks and laid on a flirtatious smile which dripped like a succulent honeycomb.

"I don't believe we've met. I'm Lexi. These are my best friends, Jess and Ariel … I mean Amy." She gestured at them. "We were inviting Jewel to the welcome back party I'm having tonight. You simply must come, Jewel. And bring your new friend." Her false lashes brushed her cheeks as she smiled at me in all her phoniness.

"I assure you I will not. So you can stop with the crap, Lexi. You're not my friend." I removed myself from Kaiden's embrace. Desiring to put her in my rearview mirror, I plunged my shaking key into the lock of my door.

Lexi's cheeks burned with embarrassment at my snub. But unlike me, she was quick on her feet and applied a speedy comeback.

"Don't pay her no mind, Kaiden. She has a tendency to be a bit moody." She contrived a bright smile. "Well, you can come tonight without her if you want. No need for you both to be party poopers. Besides, I can introduce you to more appealing acquaintances. What do you say?"

Kaiden watched her intently before serving her a dry reply. "As I said, I have plans with Jewel. And I've got things to attend to at home."

"Suit yourself." Lexi shrugged her shoulders. "Your loss, pretty boy." She blew him a kiss before pivoting on her bright yellow high heels and clicking off. Followed by her two hemorrhoids.

Kaiden gawked after them for a moment longer. Turning to me with a shake of his head, he said, "There always has to be those type of girls in every school, doesn't there?"

"Yup and they always seem to find me." I opened my door and threw my stuff on the passenger seat.

I straightened and glanced back at him to find his eyes fixated on me. He was suffocatingly close, and I swallowed the lump constricting in the hollow of my throat.

"What?" I breathed out a whisper.

"You are aware of why those girls and girls like them dislike you so much, right?" he asked, resting an arm on the roof of my car.

I fought the urge to move him out of my personal bubble. Rooting my feet in their current position, I answered him. "Oh, I've been enlightened of people's perspective on the matter. But if this were true, why do teachers also find ways to demean me? Don't get me wrong, I've had my share of amazing teachers, but I have had ones who single me out with the intent of squashing my spirit."

"Some teachers seem to be here just to collect a paycheck," he said with a shake of his head.

"Yeah, I guess. Listen, thanks for popping up when you did. You were the angel I needed at the moment."

"Angel? Now, that's a word I've never been called before." He placed a hand on his jaw as he threw the word around in his head.

"There is a first for everything," I exulted as I slid in behind my steering wheel. The scent of my tropical Hawaiian breeze air freshener hit me. I gleamed up at him. "It was a pleasure to meet you, Kaiden. I look forward to seeing you around."

He had a way about him that made me feel at ease. I almost dared believe … safe?

"So what, no playing catch?" He lifted his brow.

"Not today. I have riding lessons tonight."

"Sweet. You have a motorbike?" His eyes glinted with excitement.

"A four-legged bike that resembles a horse," I informed him with a smirk.

"Okay, I will let you go. I'll see you around?"

"Yes, for sure." I smiled, sending him a small wave, and closed my door.

As I drove out of the parking lot, I watched him in my rearview mirror. Like he was expecting I would, he lifted a hand to wave as I left.

Kaiden Carter, what are you all about?

# CHAPTER FIVE

*Kaiden*

A sliver of a smile remained on my face as her blues met mine in her rearview mirror. Currents seized my veins, and my heart skipped a beat or two or three.

Only moments ago, I caught a glimpse into Jewel's desolate school life. You would have to be a lame brain not to see the rivalry mirrored in Lexi's face as her eyes combed over Jewel. I'd observed girls like her before and made sure to steer clear of them. Girls like her thought they were the alphas of the school, and their mission was to prey on the weak. Or in Jewel's case, Lexi saw something in her that made her feel inadequate.

I'd gotten a VIP ticket to what Jewel endured as a beautiful girl living in a girl-crazed competitive world. Yet somehow, Jewel radiated an enticing humbleness. She seemed to be a "what you see is what you get" kind of girl. She wasn't artificial. No silly head games. She was simply her.

Her car had long disappeared when an angry car horn jarred me out of my musings.

"Come on, buddy, move out of the middle of the road," a yell came from the car that sounded like it may be on its last leg.

I swerved to find a car which didn't appear to be from this decade. Rust ate at its blue exterior. The guy sitting behind the wheel arched his head out the window, his arm resting on the window ledge of his dented door.

"Sorry, my apologies," I stepped back out of the path of his hunk of junk.

The dark complexioned guy frowned at my reply.

"No worries. Are you new?" His dark eyes clouded with questioning.

"Yes, I recently moved here with my mom."

He tilted his neck in the direction Jewel had gone in. "Jewel … do you know her from before?"

What was with this guy and his grilling?

"I met her a time or two why?" I asked, coyly.

"No reason. But to give you the heads-up, she isn't your kind of girl."

"Excuse me?" I glared at him wholly irritated.

"Jewel is different than most. She is good. She won't go for someone like you."

"Are you like the Jewel police or something?" My eyes narrowed, and my blood seethed at his integration.

"Look, I don't know you, but you appear to be the badass or jock type. Jewel is a girl of quality. I don't mean any offense, I'm only saying I've known her all my life, and she doesn't like your type," he said, sliding his black framed glasses back up his nose with his index finger.

"So are you her protector or something?" I retorted with a frosty bite.

"No, of course not. Jewel and I aren't even friends. But I know the war she fights every day, and I'm not going to let a guy like you put the final nail in her coffin. Why don't you leave her be?"

Who was this guy? Was he trying to state his ownership on the mysterious blonde we stood in the emptying parking lot arguing over? Maybe she was into the nerdy type?

"I assure you …"

"It's Finn. Finn Gracia," he asserted with a jut of his chin and an icy stare.

"I'm Kaiden Carter." I extended a hand to him. "Let me set it to you straight. I can appreciate you looking out for Jewel, but let me assure you I have no ill intent."

"Umm, okay," he stumbled, offering his hand.

"Maybe we can start this introduction over." I grinned, gesturing a hand back and forth.

Finn waited for a moment longer before offering a wide smile. "We can do that."

"Great."

"I've got to run. You have yourself a good one." He waved a half-wave, and his car spit and sputtered out of the parking lot.

Once again, I was left to be viewed through a rearview mirror. And for the second time, I offered the fading wave.

I pressed the code into the digital keypad of the front door of my current home. Turning the handle, I pushed the door open with my foot while performing a balancing act with my books and the brown paper bag of groceries my mom had requested I pick up after school.

The humming of instrumental ballads resonated from the built-in speakers in the cathedral ceiling. Sleek white marble floors expanded the foyer and led to the kitchen. The clanging and banging of pots and dishes coming from the kitchen clued me in to my mom's whereabouts.

Entering the rustic gray-colored kitchen, I found her. She stood at the sink overlooking the backyard. Piles of soap suds spilled over on the white and gray-veined marble countertops. My mom was elbow deep in suds, washing dishes. Her hips swayed side to side to the rhythm of the music as her voice strummed the words to the song. Her black dress slacks were pressed with care and paired with a blush-colored short-sleeve cashmere sweater. Her blond bob was styled neatly.

Today was a good day. I breathed a sigh of contentment.

"Hey, Mom," I called out, dropping the grocery bag on the counter before unloading my books on the barstool at the kitchen island.

Mom turned, and a smile lit her clear eyes. "Kaiden, honey, I didn't hear you come in." She wiped her hands on a blue hand towel.

I rounded the counter and planted a kiss on her forehead. She gazed up at me, and a frown tugged at her brow line. I recognized the familiar look of guilt.

I wrapped my arms around her, and she rested her head on my chest.

"I love you, Mom." I encouraged, softly caressing her back.

"I love you too, son." She paused a moment longer in my embrace before she pressed back.

She produced a cheerful smile once more on her lightly powdered face. "I see you got what I asked for?" She pointed at the abandoned grocery bag.

"Yes. By the way, what's for supper?"

"Your favorite." She grinned, and a single dimple etched into her right cheek.

"Pizza?" I mused, unloading the groceries on the counter.

She curled a fist and waved it in the air in a playful display of distress. "Pad Thai."

"Sounds great. Anything I can help with?"

"No. I would like my handsome son to sit and chat with me while I prepare supper. We don't get good days often, do we?" Her shoulders slumped as she turned to retrieve a cutting board. Depression may take her in and out of dealing with reality, but when she was well, she openly admitted her failings as a mother.

Only months ago, our family home went into foreclosure. Mom hadn't worked since my dad's death, and the savings ran out. Though I found a part-time job after school, it wasn't enough to keep up with the mortgage payment. The daunting look on her face as we stood out front of the home that last day dug at me. Her words charred into my mind. " Kai, I'm sorry I let you down. You lost your dad and your mom. It's not fair. You deserve better. I want to get better... I do. I have to. I've wasted so much time in that bed. I promise you I will do whatever it takes." The past years had engraved deep aging lines into her once youthful face.

From the back seat of my grandparents' Town Car, I'd reached for her trembling hand and covered it with mine. As we drove away, I turned to look out the window to hide the tears. People speak of a rock bottom, and that day was ours. The death of my dad broke my once strong and reliable mom. The loss of our home, as detrimental as it was, somehow snapped her back.

"How was your first day?" she asked as her head disappeared inside the stainless steel fridge.

"It was good. Better than I expected. Same as all the rest of the schools. But maybe more on the posh side. A lot of spoiled, wealthy, self-entitled kids. I did meet a girl though—"

"Girl?" Mom's head peeked up over the fridge door. The mention of a girl had captured her attention as I knew it would.

I laughed at the interest nuzzling her face. "Yes, a girl. Her name is Jewel."

"Okay?" She waited, and impatience gripped at her wide-set green eyes.

I allowed a moment of dead air between us before I put her out of her misery.

"She is nice," I baited her with my noninformative reply.

"Kaiden! You'd better spill the beans I won't wait for a second longer." She came out from behind the fridge door, snapping it shut behind her. Her soft angled eyebrows knitted together. In one hand, she held a carton of eggs, and the other hand curled into a fist on her trim hip.

I snorted a laugh at her cute display of madness.

While she prepared supper, I filled her in on my first day and the beautiful girl who had stolen my attention.

# CHAPTER SIX

## Jewel

The next day, he was waiting in the school parking lot as I pulled into a parking stall. Casually, he half sat on the rusty red bike railing with his hands jammed in his front pockets. His white sneakers glistened like new against his light jeans. He wore the same brown leather jacket as yesterday, and a plain teal t-shirt peeked out from underneath. Spotting me pull in, he offered me a friendly smile, revealing his perfect teeth. *I wonder if he has any idea how hot he is?* I grasped to a small wish that maybe he was waiting for me.

I jumped out of my car and quickly locked the doors.

He glided toward me, threading a hand through his damp hair. "Morning, Jewel."

"Hey, how are you?"

He had been waiting for me! A powerful drumming generated in my guarded heart.

"Here, let me take this for you," he said, removing my backpack from my shoulder and slinging it over his.

"You don't have to. I was fine with it."

His face split into a grin. "It makes me appear manly."

I almost choked on my saliva at his remark.

"You go ahead and be manly. Don't let me stand in your way," I said with a smirk.

"Good. So if you are into the manly type, what do you say about going to the mall after school?" he mused.

"I wouldn't consider going to the mall a manly thing."

"Okay, that was a bit much." He chuckled. "The truth is, my mom's birthday is tomorrow, and I want to buy her something nice. Any chance you would want to tag along?" He crossed his arms over his chest, my eyes following his movement.

Seconds ago, I'd been contemplating if he was crazy. Now I stood lost in the glory of his fineness, stalling my reply.

"Are you going to leave a guy hanging or what?"

"Yes. I mean, I would have to ask my mom, but I'd be down for that."

"Awesome."

"Okay, I'll let you know." I nodded, crossing the grass toward the front steps. "You still haven't told me much about yourself. Do you have siblings?"

He shook his head. "No, it's just my mom and me. My dad died when I was fifteen of liver cancer. My mom never married again. She says my dad and she were soulmates and that she couldn't imagine marrying anyone else."

"I'm sorry about your dad."

"Thanks, he was pretty awesome. The kind of dad who never missed a baseball game and took me out for ice cream afterward. On the weekends, he would find some project for us to do together. It's one of the things I miss the most. This was his coat. Wearing it somehow makes me feel closer to him," he said, averting his gaze to his jacket. "I wish he were here for Mom." His voice caught for a second. "For the future and grad and stuff. All the important things in life parents should be around for."

I fought the urge to reach out and comfort him. "I can understand that."

But as fast as he opened himself up for me to peek into a vulnerable side of him, he sealed it away.

"Anyway, what about your folks? Are they together still?"

"Honestly, my folks are great. Mom and Dad are high school sweethearts. I have a twenty-year-old brother named Miles. He is quieter than I am. Maybe a wee bit of an introvert. But he is a typical brother. A pain in the butt yet I couldn't imagine life without him. He listens to my problems … things I don't necessarily want to talk to my parents about. I also have a four-year-old sister named Ellie. She is adorable and a lot of work." I smirked as I thought of my defiant kid sister.

"I always wanted a brother. Not sure why my parents never had another," he added with a shrug of his shoulders.

Reaching the front doors of the school, he stepped up and opened them. "After you, Miss Hart." He exaggerated a half-bow.

"Thanks." I laughed at his theatrics and waltzed through the doors.

At my locker, I turned to say something to him and collided with his chest. He clasped the small of my back to steady me.

"I … sorry," I blurted, unnerved by his closeness. Excitement fluttered in my chest as the warmth of his hand bit through my thin cotton shirt.

I retreated from his arms and retrieved my cell phone from my backpack.

"I'll see you at lunch?"

"You can count on it," he said. Giving me a thumbs-up and handing me my backpack, he turned and headed down the hall.

I caught sight of Lexi and her squad as they wielded him with a flirtatious woo.

"Hi, Kaiden," they sang.

He acknowledged them with a polite nod and swirled around to face me while shuffling backward.

"You and me lunch. Okay, Jewel?"

I knew what he was up to, and it stirred my already pounding heart. I bobbed my head at him and turned to put my backpack in my locker. I appealed to it to swallow me up. At this moment, if I could climb inside and padlock the door, I would.

*Please, not today. Keep walking, keep walking.*

I closed my eyes tightly, willing the universe to oblige me with this one small request. *Please don't let them taint this almost perfect morning.*

Then it happened! Pain shot through my head as my head collided with the metal of the locker. The result of a forceful shove from behind. Instinct set in and I went into defense mode.

I swiveled in anger, charged and ready to take on my attackers. Lexi stood with a satisfied smugness lining her perfectly made-up face.

I rubbed the knot threatening to form on my forehead. "Don't … don't touch me." My voice trembled.

"Or what, Hart? What could you possibly do? You and all your friends going to take us on?" She waved her hand in the air and looked side to side to find anyone who would stand up for me.

What could I do? Nothing, and they knew it. I was alone and helpless. Students had started to gather, thirsty for a fight.

Lexi dominated over me in her five-inch royal blue stilettos.

"Are you deaf, Hart?" I asked what are you going to do?" she continued her taunting.

My legs quivered and hot tingles coursed through me as I gulped back the thickening at the back of my throat.

"Lexi, come on, let's go. It's not worth it," Amy pleaded, pulling at Lexi's arm.

"Amy, shut up!" Jess spat, a devilishness glinted her gunmetal blue eyes.

"Surely, you're not going to take that from her? Are you?" Jess attempted to egg me on.

"I think you all had better get to class. Right now!" a voice bellowed. The crowd parted as Mr. B, one of the school's chem and bio teachers, stepped into the ring of students formed around us.

Lexi's eyes flashed at me, warning me it wasn't over. She pivoted and marched off, followed by her shadows.

"Go on, the rest of you. Clear out of here," Mr. B shouted.

My ballerina flats remained fixed to the ground as he turned to me.

"Care to enlighten me on what all this fuss was about?" he asked, fastening his gaze on mine. A genuine concern covered his face.

"I didn't do this. I was putting—"

"I know you aren't a scrapper or a problem maker, and most likely, you never started whatever this was. You can't allow people to treat you with disrespect. You have the right to attend this school in peace as much as the next student," he stressed.

"Trust me, Mr. B, I've been trying for years," I said with a bitter laugh. "Lexi hates me and goes out of her way to track me down."

"What happened there?" He scowled, nodding at my forehead.

"What do you think …?" I retorted, casting my eyes to the ground.

"You mean? Did she do this to you? I thought they were taunting you. She won't be getting away with that either, but I was not aware—" His words were cut off by the bell. "Get to class. I will deal with this." He twisted on his heels and marched his five-foot-self down the hallway. The fluorescent hall lights gleaming off his clean-shaved head as he went.

All morning, I fumed inside at what took place at the lockers. Why did I have to live like this? Why couldn't I catch a break? My wish for my last year to be different appeared to be dying fast.

Currently, in math class, I sat slumped forward with my cheek resting on my hand. I stared at the page assignment on my desk, which was to graph a linear function. Math continued to be my archenemy. Some people just got it, but unfortunately, that wasn't me. Math seemed like someone was speaking in a second language to me.

I focused on the graph in front of me while my mind spun. I mulled over how to make Lexi shrivel up and float away. I couldn't go through another year of this. Something needed to give. I worked hard every day to be in a healthy mind space, but I grew weary of trying to make it through the day without being mocked and attacked. A tear slid from the corner of my eye, and I promptly brushed it away. I wouldn't give Lexi this power over me.

"Jewel," Finn Gracia whispered from his seat across the aisle from me. His almost black eyes pleading with empathy.

Finn inhabited all the nice guy attributes as far as I could see. I would paint him as the nerdy type. His family arrived in Canada from Mexico when we were in grade five. I recalled his first day at school. He stood at the front of the classroom with the teacher as she introduced him to the class. He'd worn a yellow jacket and a red backpack. His thick black hair had been slicked back, and his eyes nervous and scared as he looked across the room at his gawking peers. His eyes rested on me, and I flashed him the best smile I could muster. Over the years, we chatted and had been friendly, but it was as far as it went.

"I heard about Lexi and her gang of followers. Don't let them get you down. That's what they want. They want to break you."

"I know, Finn." A case of melancholy engulfed me.

"It's them, not you. There is nothing wrong with you," he said, darting his eyes to check if the teacher was aware of his chatter. But she sat behind her desk engrossed in her laptop.

"Thank you." I smiled earnestly.

He nodded and went back to his work.

Of course, the incident spread like wildfire. Students loved gossip and all too often thrived on fights and drama. Was it too much to ask to be left alone? I looked around at the pale blue wall of what had become my prison. Two days in and my cellmates had successfully chipped away at my spirit. There was no hope in this place. The only hope I found was when I walked out those front doors.

At the end of class, Mr. B met me in the hall.

"Hey, Jewel I wanted to let you know I informed the principal of Lexi's attack on you. He promised to see to it."

"Thanks, Mr. B, but I won't hold my breath for him to actually follow through with anything. If he attempts to, I'm sure it will only be a gentle slap on the wrist. For some reason, my efforts and my parents' efforts to involve the authority at school have been in vain. We've had the sit-downs with the parents and staff. And minutes after leaving the office, the kids continue with their previous behavior."

"I know what you and your family are feeling. I get it. My son has also dealt with bullying, and you guys shouldn't have to. I want to make a difference for you and for him. I will keep trying, Jewel, and my door is always open. Okay?"

"Thanks, Mr. B. I appreciate you caring." My heart warmed at the kind smile he offered me.

"You're a good kid, Jewel. Don't let them hold you down," he said as he turned to head back to his classroom across the hall.

# CHAPTER SEVEN

*Jewel*

S chool ended, and I was liberated from the confining chains as I sprang out the double doors. My feet were eager to flee the reformatory behind their barricades. The excitement of another day ending sounded as students fell in step around me.

I welcomed the affection of the sun as it gingerly kissed my cheeks.

*Let freedom reign.* I breathed in pure bliss.

The screech of rubber meeting pavement pierced the air. We turned our eyes to the white Porsche racing out of the lot.

Chad. Go figure. Complete moron. I bristled.

I regarded my peers. Girls and guys alike ogled him with a sickening obsession. Some shook their heads as if they expected nothing more of him. The students with half a brain looked on in distaste.

I spotted Kaiden through the crowd engaged in

conversation with Finn.

Of all people. I smiled, approving his choice in friends. A nerd like Finn and a loner like me were the ones he chose to socialize with. Popularity didn't appear to be at the forefront of his agenda, and this gesture picked away at the mold around my heart. I gathered some courage and wandered over to join them.

"Jewel, hey," Finn greeted. His friendly, inviting face and his laid-back mannerisms instantly put me at ease. Finn was average height with a thickening waistline from too much of his mom's cooking. A problem which needed solving to him was like sugar was to me.

"Hello, Finn, Kaiden."

"Kai," Kaiden reminded me.

"All right, you got it. Kai, it is." I glanced into his summoning dark eyes. As he reached out and brushed a tendril of my hair behind my ear, a powerful jolt rippled through my body.

"Hey, guys, not to interrupt this frozen in time moment between you, but I'm still here," Finn teased, adjusting the green backpack slung over his shoulder. The braces on his straightening teeth glistening in the sunlight.

My fingers tightened on my backpack, and I looked away. A hot breeze rushed through me at Finn's comment. "I'm going to head home. I'll catch you two around."

"No, wait, Jewel. Don't go," Finn protested in distress. "Dammit! There I go, ruining everything." He stamped his foot in frustration.

I guffawed, brushing off his fretting. " Don't go wasting any of your brain cells over that. You did nothing wrong. I need to grab Ellie from daycare, and I only have twenty minutes after the dismissal bell rings. So, as you can see, everything isn't about you, Finn," I jested.

He rewarded me with an infectious smile that etched into his rounded cheeks. "Fine, I'll believe your lie," he chorused back.

"All right, got to run. Later."

My engine sputtered to a start as a knock echoed on my window, sending my heart into the hollow of my throat. Turning, I saw Kaiden crouched down to eye level with me and signaling for me to roll the window down.

I clicked the button and reached to turn down the music. "Hey, what's up?"

"Bublé girl, are ya?"

"Yes, I enjoy his music. I believe him to be the modern day Frank Sinatra." I scanned the arm he placed on the edge of my door. "But that isn't why you are here. How can I be of service?"

"I wanted to remind you about maybe going to the mall later tonight," he said. His eyes trailed over my face, wavering on my mouth, and his chest rose and fell with rapid breaths.

"I will run it by my mom, but I don't see her having an issue with it. She gets home around five, but until then, I have to watch my sister. How about we exchange numbers, and I will text you when I speak to her? Does that work for you?" I twisted the diamond stud in my left earlobe.

He rocked back on his heels, closed his eyes, and raised one hand to the sky. "Thank you, God. I finally get her number." He looked back at me, his eyes bouncing with mischievousness. "You know it's halfway through the week, and I've been waiting since we met at the coffee shop to get your number." His laugh was charming and contagious as he stood.

Retrieving his cell from his back pocket, he typed the number I recited to him into it.

"You are something else." I laughed. "So sure of yourself, aren't you?" I watched him in amazement at the confidence exuding from him.

Some might describe him as cocky, and he did appear to be exactly that. But why did I get the sense there was more to him than what first met the eye?

His smile wavered, and he muttered, "Everything isn't always as it seems."

"What do you mean?"

He stood. "I mean, one foot in front of the other has become my motto most days. Sometimes, life sucks really bad, but we have to force ourselves to go on. Life requires some of us to grow up faster than others. Somedays, I want to stay in bed and never get up. Somedays, I want to kick shit because it would simply make me feel better, and sometimes, I give in to the urge. But I don't like feeling that way, and I refuse to live my life like that. Put all this aside, and I feel you are a girl worth fighting for." He looked away, and with a light tap on the side of my car, he backed up. "You'd best get going." He plunged his hands deep into his jean pockets. "I'll see you around." His body hunched forward as he turned and walked away.

"Okay," I mumbled to myself.

I clicked the button to roll up my window and pulled out of the parking lot. My thoughts ran over the little I knew about him. He was charming and acted so sure of himself. But I was sure now this wasn't the case. He revealed a side to me which rang true to my belief that he was kind of broken like the rest of us.

## Kaiden

For the second time in a week, I stood watching her leave. Without warning, flashbacks of what my life used to be like dragged me back. As they overtook me, I shut down and shut her out.

Jewel awakened feelings in me I had never experienced before. She was a glimmer of light in the lethal storm engrossing my life. She stirred a vulnerability in me that thrilled and frightened me in the same juncture.

In my desire to hide my problems at home, I had isolated myself from friends, which led to detaching myself from the world. But within weeks, Jewel become an assurance I knew I needed. *This can't be normal? But do I even know what normal is anymore? Am I not a fraud to myself and her with my display of strength?*

Three years ago, I'd come to a crossroads and was faced with the choice to either join my mom in her spiraling hole of sinking sand or to survive. Had my world not been shattered enough with the loss of the man who'd kept our family strong? Who was I kidding; I could never be him.

Fate decided to push me further. Months after his passing, I'd come home to find Mom grasping onto her last breath. Alarm engulfed me when I didn't find her in her room. I raced from room to room, yelling out for her. In the kitchen, lying on the counter, I found a folded note with my name scribbled on the front.

"No, no, you don't!" I slammed my fist on the counter. "Mom?" My scream resounded throughout the kitchen.

Fear gutted me.

The day my mom tried to take her life remained the worst day of my life. Losing my dad devastated us both, but the fact she would choose to leave me … Where was her fight? She was the parent. We were supposed to comfort each other. Because I lost him too.

I found her limp body in my dad's chair in his den. Her body collapsed against his desk. She wore his white dress shirt and a pair of underwear. The empty pill bottle smirked at me from where it lay toppled over on the desk. Her once long blond hair lay unwashed, concealing her face from me. Tears of utter despair blinded me as I crept toward her.

I brushed back her hair to see her face, and I noticed the shallow rise and fall of her back.

"Mom?" My voice clogged.

Calling the dreaded 911, the voice of the operator echoed over the phone.

"911. What is your emergency?"

"Hi … my mom, she tried … she tried to kill herself," I mumbled into the phone as the room began to spin.

Their arrival became a blur. At the hospital, she was put on suicide watch. My grandparents came to stay with me. Mom remained at the hospital for a week until they deemed she was not a threat to herself. My grandparents stayed with us for a few months. Mom's parents tried to urge her to come and stay with them, but she refused to leave all the memories our town and home held of my dad. My grandparents left me with strict orders to keep them updated.

"Kai?" she said one night as I lay on the couch, trying to block out my worries with the distraction of an episode of *Gotham*.

"Yes?"

"I'm sorry, baby." Tears glistened in her eyes. Guilt consumed her, and she evaded my gaze. "I'm sorry for the burden I have placed on you. I can't seem to live without him. He has been part of my life since we were children. I know in my head I have to overcome this and go on for you. I've always considered myself a strong woman, but now I realize he was my strength and my rock. Together we were a team."

I stared at the TV, listening to her fidget while she waited for my reply. The TV screen faded as I considered her words. Finally, I looked at her, and through gritted teeth, I asked, "Do you think it's all peachy from where I'm sitting? I'm the kid, Mom, but I'm the one picking up the pieces. Am I not part of the team?"

"Yes, you were. You are." She buried her face in her hands and wept.

I wanted her to snap the hell out of it. At that moment, I couldn't stand the sounds of her sobs. Bitterness at my situation ate at me.

"Please, Kaiden. Don't turn on me. I will try. I promise I will."

I didn't want to push her back to where she was a few months ago. Fear of being without both my parents strangled me. That night, I decided to bury my feelings and the memories of my dad. Thinking of him had been too hard for us. I made a choice to be the strength he'd once been for her. In doing so, I stopped living the life of a teen.

# CHAPTER EIGHT

*Lexi*

"Chad, slow the hell down." Lexi glared at him from the passenger seat as Chad ripped from the parking lot. The smell of burnt rubber reached her nose from the marks he left on the pavement. His ear-bleeding rap music vibrated through the car.

Chad's blue eyes glinted with the thrill and need for speed. Pulling out of the school, he raced out into the street and accelerated well past the speed limit.

Her knuckles whitened as she gripped the door handle. Chad glanced over at her and delighted in the fear in her eyes as they tore down the street. Her fear only heightened his recklessness. His eyes shot back to the road as two pedestrians' feet hit the crosswalk in front of them. He hit his brakes, and the sudden stop launched Lexi forward, her hands grasping the front dash to keep her head from hitting the windshield.

In a daze, she glanced around. The two pedestrians who'd jumped back on the sidewalk yelled and cursed at Chad and give him the finger. With a shake of their heads, they crossed the street.

"You're so stupid, Chad," Lexi said hotly, rubbing the back of her neck to ease the pain from the sudden stop.

"Shut up!" His eyes shot daggers at her as the car started rolling again.

"You'll kill someone someday, and then it will be all over for you."

"I told you to shut the hell up." He reached out and backhanded her across the side of the face.

A gasp and a half-cry escaped her.

Chad grew annoyed and gave her a shove, cracking her temple against the window.

"Stop it!" she cried through welling tears.

"Keep your mouth shut. I don't need you scolding me and treating me like a child." He sharply took the corner of the next street and immediately geared up, charging down the street.

Lexi ceased her cries and turned to look out the window. She hated him most days. Chad was abusive and cruel, but he looked good on her arm and helped raise her status quo, so for this reason, she stayed. With him, she and he could rule the school, and in this, it gave her a sense of control over her own life. As long as she was on top, it would assure this. It played on her mind the fact she knew he had cheated on her and more than once.

But she was used to shitty men in her life. Starting with the one man who was supposed to be there for her. Her dad. She had considered herself a daddy's girl until he walked out a few years ago without so much as a goodbye. Things had always been rocky between her mom and dad. *The night he left, a fight had broken out between them, and Lexi arrived home in the middle of it. As she entered the house through the garage door, their loud voices sent her hurrying down the hall to the kitchen.*

*"Please, Dan, don't go. I need you," her mom begged.*

*"I can't stand to be here another moment with you. The sight of you repulses me," Lexi's dad seethed.*

*"That isn't true. You love me. I know you do." She rounded the corner in time to see her mom grip his arm in desperation.*

*"No, I don't love you. We're over. I can't do this anymore."*

*"It's the other woman, isn't it? The blonde one. The whore has broken up my family," she accused as he shook her off his arm.*

*"No, it's not her. That is over and has been for a while, so you can stop surmising."*

*"Get out, you bastard! You only ever cared for Lexi anyway," she said with a nasty twist of her face.*

*"You got that right. If it weren't for her, I would've been gone years ago," he shouted.*

*"Leave! But I warn you. You will never lay eyes on your daughter again. I will do what it takes to turn her against you. She will hate the ground you walk on."*

*"Fuck off, Erin," he said with a snarl. Grabbing his keys from the counter, he turned and his eyes livid and fueled with anger fell on Lexi. He gulped back a breath and muzzled a groan as he pushed past her.*

*"Dad. Stop. Don't go." Lexi ran after him, grabbing at the back of his coat, but he jerked himself free. "Please, Dad. Don't listen to her. She is just mad. You guys can work through it."*

*He sailed through the garage door and slammed the door shut behind him. He was gone without a word or a second look. Her heart crumbled, and she sobbed. Resting her forehead against the door, she pounded on it with her fist. "No, no, no ... please come back." But he didn't. He disappeared altogether.* Except for the child support check which appeared every month, her dad became a ghost, and her pathetic weak mother was the only person to blame.

With her dad's disappearance, her mom frequented the bars, and men came in and out of her life. Lexi became low on her priority list, and during these times, she turned to the only person who appeared to care. Jewel. They had started a friendship a few months before this all went down with Lexi's family. Jewel had it all—the perfect family and the perfect life. Everything Lexi wanted and would never have. Jewel was the beautiful blonde who turned heads like the blonde who had turned Lexi's dad's. A seed of jealousy started to sprout in her over those next few months after her dad left. It wasn't fair. She began to loathe Jewel for all she had and what she could only dream of having.

One day as they lounged in Jewel's backyard by her pool, she looked at her lying on her lounger in her cute little teal bikini with her flat stomach. Her diamond belly button ring sparkled in the sunlight. Lexi looked down at her slightly fuller stomach with her recent weight gain.

Lexi peered at Jewel through her sunglasses and said, "You are getting a little hefty around your stomach, Jewel."

Jewel turned to look at her. "What?" She placed her hands on her stomach in an effort to conceal herself.

"I mean, it's not too bad, but I've noticed. Lately, you have gained some weight."

Jewel sat up. "Really? But the scales don't say that," she said meekly, swallowing hard.

"You may need to change the battery or get a new set. I didn't want to say anything, but people have started to notice." She voiced her own truth as she took a long sip of her ice-cold lemonade.

"But …" Jewel's lip quivered.

"I wouldn't cry over it or anything. I'm supposed to tell you this stuff. I'm your friend."

Jewel choked back her tears. The notch Lexi carved out of Jewel's self-esteem pleased her. Lexi settled back against her lounger with a smirk etched on her face.

"I'll be right back," Jewel murmured.

Moments later, she returned wearing a long sleeve shirt and a pair of shorts. Lexi laughed to herself and her spirits lifted as Jewel's self-esteem plummeted. Seeing someone else's pain shadowed the pain of neglect and worthlessness she felt. In this, Lexi became the puppet master and Jewel became her puppet.

# Chad

Lexi slammed the door as she got out of his car. She started for the house before turning and stalking back toward the car her arms swinging at her sides as she went. She stopped on Chad's side of the car. Drawing back her foot, she kicked the door with all her might. He heard the dent her foot put in the door before he threw open his door to investigate the damage. Lexi charged for the house with him right on her heels.

"I'm going to kill you, you little bitch," he yelled.

Lexi raced up the front steps into the house, swiftly closing and locking the door. Chad's fist echoed against the wooden door.

"You will need to face me sometime, Lexi," he shouted before storming back to see the damage she'd done to his car. His jaw twitched, and he cursed the large dent.

He jumped into his car and threw it in gear, then driving his car to the middle of the lawn, he stopped. Revving up the motor, he spun his tires and sent grass and dirt flying everywhere. He hit the gas and his car thrashed over the sidewalk and back on the street. "That will teach her. She can explain that one to her mom," he said with a snicker.

He pulled his car into his driveway ten minutes later. His dad's black Aston Martin Vanquish pulled in behind him. Chad lived in the nicest house in the community. The size of his ten-bedroom, eight-bathroom mansion was excessive for his family of three. He clicked the garage opener on his visor, and the first door of their seven-car garage moved up. He ripped his car inside the garage. His dad's and his addiction for fast cars filled every stall. From Lamborghini to a Maserati GranTurismo, the Palmers owned it all.

"Hey, Dad," Chad greeted as his father got out of his car.

"I want the deal finished by the end of the day. No more excuses, Roger. Make sure it's a signed deal," his dad said into his cell phone while shooting Chad a half-wave. "I don't care what it takes. You can kiss your holidays goodbye if you don't make this deal happen today. Now get it done." He pulled the phone from his ear and clicked end. He reached into his car and retrieved his sports coat and briefcase from the passenger seat.

"Look what Lexi did to my car." Chad gestured toward

his car door.

"What?" His dad flipped through his phone preoccupied.

"I said look at what Lexi did to my car."

His dad glanced up, and his eyes turned to where Chad pointed. "Why did she do that?" he said in an even tone as his eyes turned back to his phone.

"Because she gets like this sometimes."

"We will sort this out. Run down to the body shop and have them give you a quote and you can give it to her."

Chad laughed, "As if she will pay for it."

"Sure, whatever. You can pay for it then. Look, are we done here? I have things to attend to."

"Whatever, Dad," Chad retorted.

His dad walked out of the garage and disappeared around the corner of the house.

"I'll see you next month," Chad said with a grumble for his ears only. His phone chimed alerting him of a text message. He tapped in his code to read it.

Lexi says: *I'm sorry, baby.*

He texted back: *You'd better be. You are paying for the damages.*

Lexi replies: *I can't afford to. I will make it up to you with special favors.* She followed her text with a kissing face emoji.

A smile broke across his face. You're right, you will. You will give me what I need and whatever else I want. His mind played with the ideas of what exactly he would require from her to make up for fucking up his car.

Another text rang through, but this time it was from Dillon.

Dillion says: *Got your quota.*

Chad: *Sweet. I could use a little excitement in my night.*

*Meet you same time and same place?*

Dillon: *Yup.*

Chad tucked his phone in the back pocket of his jeans. Adrenaline coursed through his body. He moved to the garage washroom, and inside, he lifted the back off the toilet and removed the baggie of white substance taped underneath the lid. His step was lighter, and his dark mood faded as he went into the house with the intent of achieving his next high.

# CHAPTER NINE

*Jewel*

Ellie was a royal crank pot when I picked her up from daycare. Her ear-piercing screams filled the car the entire car ride home.

Now, she stood pinned to my legs as I struggled to open the front door. My arms were overloaded with her belongings and mine. She tucked one arm between my legs and wrapped it around my knee. Her head of honey blond curls rested like a dead weight against me. Her little body convulsing softly as she breathed in and out. Tuckered out from her tantrum, she stood quietly with her thumb in her mouth.

Success. The door unlocked as the load in my arms tumbled to the ground.

"Okay, Ellie, in you go. Sissy's got to pick this stuff up."

"But I want you to hold me," she fussed, her tired blue eyes started to water.

Great. My nerves were beginning to wear thin.

"I will once we are inside. I need you to be a big girl and go inside."

At the reference to her being a big girl, her eyes brightened, and she stomped inside. As she walked ahead, I realized she was missing one of her pink sandals. In her hysterics, she must have thrown it somewhere in my car.

I dropped my keys into the mosaic-tiled bowl my parents bought on our recent trip to Thailand. The bowl sat in the center of the mirrored glass stand in the main entry. Wandering down to the mudroom, I put Ellie's jacket and backpack into her assigned cubby hole.

In the kitchen, I unpacked her lunch kit and washed out the containers then deposited the kit in the corner of the counter out of sight.

Ellie wandered into the kitchen with the baby blanket she faithfully hauled around.

"Do you want a juice box?" I asked.

With her thumb still popped in her mouth, she sauntered over to the double-wide stainless steel built-in fridge and tugged open the door. Her sweaty fingers leaving their imprint.

After five minutes of her trying to decide what she wanted for a snack, I got her settled at the kitchen island.

Retrieving my phone, I glanced at it.

One missed text.

I didn't recognize the number. Swiping the screen to view it, I felt a smile tug immediately at the corners of my mouth as I read it.

He texted. *Hey, Beauty, missing your face already.*

Kaiden.

I texted back. *You know this might be considered stalking behavior?*

His reply was instant. *Or... it may be considered I simply like you.*

I laughed aloud, and Ellie asked, "What, Jules? What are you laughing at?" She fidgeted and leaned across the counter, trying to view my phone.

I chuckled at her attempt to see what was so funny. Like she could even read it if she could see it.

"A friend. He is being silly," I replied.

Friend? Were we friends?

"But you're a girl. You aren't supposed to have a boy as a friend," she insisted as her perfectly pink lips formed around her straw.

"What makes you think girls can't be friends with boys?" I gazed at her affectionately, leaning my elbows on the counter.

"Because you marry boys. When I grow up, I'm going to marry Miles," she said firmly with a raise of her eyebrow.

Laughter shook me until my stomach stitched with pain. "Ellie, you can't marry, Miles. He is your brother."

Insulted at my laughter, she drew down her brows and crossed her arms snugly across her chest. "You can't tell me who I can marry, Jules."

"Oh, this is how you are going to be?" I smirked at the little spitfire in front of me. "You're right, Ellie. I can't tell you who you can marry."

My phone binging reminded me of missed texts. Four new messages from Kaiden.

Kaiden: *Did I scare you off?*

*Hello?*

*Are you ignoring me?*

*I'm dying over here.*

Me: *Still here. Patience is a good trait. Maybe one you should work on.* I added an emoji with a stuck-out tongue.

Kaiden: *Oh, good, you are still alive. I was wondering if my charm had made you faint or something.* He added the emoji with hearts for eyes.

Me: *You're extreme.*

Kaiden: *I know. Okay, in all seriousness. If your folks are okay with you going, I'll pick you up at 6:30. We could have crappy food court food for our first date.*

My heart skipped a beat. First date?

I replied: *I will text. Chat soon.*

I laid my phone on the counter. Rounding the island, I swirled Ellie from her stool and swung her in the air. She squealed in delight. Lowering her into my arms, I adjusted her on my hip. She rested her head on my shoulder, and like a retraction string was attached to her thumb, it found its way back into her mouth.

"What do you say about us snuggling on the couch and watching some cartoons?"

Against my shoulder, she bobbed her head up and down in agreement.

His shiny black sports car pulled into our driveway at exactly six thirty sharp. Hiding behind my curtains in my room, I observed him. He wavered a minute and looked up as if he sensed he was being watched. His eyes scanned over my window, and I ducked out of view.

I closed my eyes, tightly blowing out an annoyed breath.

*Good job, let him think you are some pathetic lovestruck girl.*

The chime of the doorbell sent me hurrying from my room. I made my way across the catwalk toward the spiraling stairs. The open concept of our home allowed me to survey the situation below.

"Hello, you must be Kaiden," Mom said.

"Please don't embarrass me," I breathed to myself as I reached the stairs.

I peered through the railing to see Mom had changed from her office wear and now wore a pair of black yoga pants which showed off her voluptuous figure. She was swallowed up by her pink hoodie. I'm short like her. She and I were similar in most ways except I'd inherited my dad's hair and eyes.

"Yes, Mrs. Hart. It's a pleasure to meet you." Kaiden charmed her with a dazzling smile, offering his hand in a handshake.

"You can call me Natalia, or Nat works best," Mom gushed at his well-mannered response. "Do come in. Jewel will be right down."

Kaiden peered over Mom's ponytailed head and captured me in his approving eyes as he stepped inside.

I wiped my sweaty palms on my white jeans. A warmness filled my cheeks at his open gaze. My shoulders curled forward, and an involuntary slight movement took over my hips and a sway set in.

*Good God. Get a grip.*

Mom turned and caught sight of me. "Oh, here she is. I didn't hear you come down. Well, I will let you two be on your way. It was nice to meet you, Kaiden." A smile crinkled her eyes and nose.

"Same here." Kaiden nodded. His eyes circled back to me, and he asked, "You ready?"

"Yup," I said before turning to Mom. "We will be back by the time the mall closes at the latest."

"All right, sweetheart. Have fun, you two," she said with a hum. She spun loosely on her heels and disappeared into the kitchen to finish making supper.

I was thankful Miles and Dad weren't home to embarrass me. Without a doubt, they would have made it an introduction of torment and teasing. I slipped on my waist-length black leather jacket and tucked my gold sheen wallet under my arm. "Let's go."

"After you." He gestured a hand toward the door.

My smile widened.

Nice. His mom raised him right.

I scooted past him and floated out the door. At his car, he hurried to open the door for me.

Yup, he was on a mission to rack up points. I grinned, letting him know I was on to him.

He smirked. Closing the door after me, he circled the perimeter of the car to the driver's side.

As he climbed in behind the steering wheel, I caught a wisp of soap. The fresh essence of the tantalizing tartness of lime with undernotes of sweetness sang to my senses.

I rested my head against the sleek black leather seat. His car was a far cry nicer than mine was. "Nice car. I've never seen you in it, so I thought maybe you rode a pedal bike or something," I joked, casting him a sideways glance.

"It was a gift from my grandparents." He chuckled good-naturedly at my dig.

We cruised down the street and out of my neighborhood.

I gazed out my window at the beautifully designed houses and their painstakingly groomed front yards as they passed by.

I wondered about our sudden departure from school today and decided to ask him about it.

"Earlier at school, did I do something?"

"What do you mean?" he said with a frown.

"We were talking, and it was like you shut down." I twisted to look at him.

His expression turned grim as he said, "Nah, it wasn't anything you did. I sometimes get caught up in some tough times in my life, and like you said, I shut down." Glancing at me as his hand shifted the gears, he went on, "You could say I'm fighting some demons of my own."

"It's understandable after everything you have been through. With the loss of your dad and all." I sucked in a breath of relief and lightly exhaled. I heard Mile's voice in my head, *Everything, isn't about you, Jewel.*

Reaching into my pocket, I fetched my nude lip gloss and blindly applied it to my lips. The gratifying tingle of the lip plumper puckered my lips. "I'm not going to lie. I did wonder if I said or did something wrong. But that's before I decided on the mindset that it was you with the issue, not me," I stated honestly, throwing him a wicked grin.

He slapped the stirring wheel, and his laughter at my comment echoed throughout the car "God, you are my kind of girl. Good way to lighten the mood."

My mouth hinted a smile, and I relaxed back against my seat.

Yorkdale mall was a madhouse of shoppers for a weeknight. Tonight, it appeared to be a grand central station for teens. Numerous shopping bags accented their arms and glee broadcasted across their faces. On a high from their recent purchases, the hum of happy shoppers could be heard. Shoppers rode up and down the escalators on the hunt for their next hot purchase. Shop windows advertised discounts and promotions in bold neon banners. Faceless manikins dressed in the latest fashions were displayed in each store's windows.

We headed to the first of many jewelry stores in search of the perfect necklace for Kaiden's mom. The last one we entered, a lady with overprocessed brassy blond hair who appeared to be in her fifties greeted us with a flat, disconnected voice.

"Welcome," she said before turning back to washing the glass display countertops. Rows of rings lined her stubby fingers.

Irritation chewed at me at her dismissal of us before we had barely crossed the threshold of the store. She had been all too sure of the fact two teenagers weren't going to make a sale worth her time.

I tried to cool the bristling fire in my eyes, but concealing my emotions often proved to be my weakness. They paraded across my face for an audience to see. If the woman's back had not been turned, she would have gotten a front row seat to my scowl.

Kaiden seemed to be unmarked by her rudeness.

I followed him from showcase to showcase, looking at the collections within. From custom jewelry to true Canadian diamonds.

He pointed at a beautiful necklace with a heart-shaped

diamond pendant, and in the center of the framed heart lay the designer's signature sapphire. He marveled down at the piece. "This is nice. Isn't it?"

"It's really pretty."

I wondered if he knew the value of the necklace? I was familiar with this particular collection, and it wasn't priced at a teen-friendly budget.

From the back of the store, an older, lanky African American man appeared. He bore a close resemblance to Morgan Freeman. He glanced at us with an inviting smile. "Good evening, what can I help you two with?" he asked as he came to stand in front of us. Unlike his co-worker, he was eager to offer his services.

We were the store's only patrons at the moment. The man with a name tag stating his name as "Walter" gave us his full attention.

"We are looking for a birthday present. I'm thinking of that necklace." Kaiden pointed at the necklace which caught his eye.

"Beautiful choice." Walter nodded approvingly. "I bought this for my wife for our fortieth wedding anniversary. She has been crowing about it ever since," he said as he took out his keys and unlocked the case. He withdrew the small velvet silver display showcasing the eye-catching piece of glistening diamonds.

Kaiden lifted the necklace and admired it in his fingers. He inquired about the price, and satisfied with Walter's answer, he said, "I will take it."

Walter glanced at me. "Is this the lucky lady?"

"No, no," I mumbled, shaking my head. "The necklace is for his mom. We are friends."

"Friends deserve gifts too. Especially a girl as striking as you are. And my God, those eyes of yours are like gems of their own." His genuine smile revealed even aging teeth. A small chip was etched out of his front tooth, giving him an extra charm.

I blushed. "Thank you, sir."

Kaiden was enjoying himself immensely as he watched me wiggle under Walter's praise.

Walter peered from Kaiden to me, and a smile parted his lips. He was having none of my insistence that we were friends. "Ahh, young love." His eyes drifted as if remembering a time in his own life.

"Like she said, it actually is for my mom. She deserves something extra special," Kaiden replied. An underlying sadness shadowed the aura around him.

We followed Walter to the cash register. Kaiden removed a worn tan wallet, which had survived a year too many.

Walter handed Kaiden his purchase, and a glimmer of pride crossed Kaiden's face as he looked at the gift in his hand.

Thanking Walter and wishing him a good evening, Kaiden turned to me.

"What do you say to a bite to eat? My treat," he said with a dance of his eyebrows.

Hopeless flirt.

I giggled. "Lead the way. If it's on you, how can I refuse."

He chuckled as we left the store.

# CHAPTER TEN

*Jewel*

A red-haired waitress with more freckles than her face could hold showed us to a booth at the back of the International Cuisine restaurant. The atmosphere of the restaurant was swank and current while the dimmed lights gave it an intimate vibe.

"The necklace is beautiful, Kai." I smiled across the table at him.

Our eyes connected. He tilted his head, and a hint of a dimple appeared in his cheek as he boldly held my gaze. "I dreamed of how Kai would sound coming from your lips," he said, coyly.

I rolled my eyes at his flirty banter. "Oh, my God. Seriously? Has that line worked for you in the past? Because that right there was a whole lot of cheesiness."

He laughed, placing a hand on his chest as if I'd wounded him. "Ouch."

A smile peeked from the corners of my lips. I sank back against the booth, gazing at the alluring guy who sat before me. The waitress arrived to ask for our drink order. I ordered a root beer, and he ordered a cola.

I studied him while twirling my fork between my fingers. "So tell me more about you, Kaiden."

He leaned forward, folding his hands on the table. "What do you want to know?"

"How about we start with, have you lived in the Toronto area all your life?"

His jaw tightened as if I struck a nerve. "Not always, Toronto. But Ontario, yes. I went to a few schools in our area after my dad died."

I waited for him to explain, but when he didn't, I clammed up, not sure what to say. Thankfully, the arrival of the waitress with our drinks relieved me of the awkwardness. In an effort to veer the conversation in what hopefully would be an acceptable topic for him.

Taking an extra-long sip of my drink, I asked, "What does fun look like to you?"

"Good question. Fun doesn't happen too often for me. But if you are referring to hobbies. Where do I begin?" He smiled. "I play the guitar. Acoustic and electric. I have a love for fixing up old cars. AC/DC is my favorite band—"

"What? That stuff gives me a headache."

He flashed me a wide grin for a second before it slipped. Looking away, he began to pick microscopic pieces of lint from the black cotton napkin laying under his utensils. His shoulders rose and fell as he started to explain. "My dad was a fan. We used to work on his old cars together, and he would have them jamming in the background, so I grew up liking them.

When my dad was alive, life was great. Along with the times working in our garage, my best memories were the vacations spent with my parents." Affection gleamed in his eyes as he reflected on his parents. He clutched his past close to his chest, but he failed to conceal the twist of pain on his face as an unidentifiable thought cantered through his mind.

Losing a parent was more than I could imagine, and my heart ached for him. To the world, he offered us a face that said, "I'm confident and don't have a care in the world." But I detected a fathomless pain was rooted at the center of him.

In an effort to shake off the rapid waterfall of gloom cascading down on us, he smiled. "What about you? Besides your four-legged friends at the ranch, what do you do in your free time?"

I twirled the ice cubes in my root beer with my straw. "Well, I'm an artsy kind of girl. Hours and hours, I etch away at a sketch pad, letting my imagination run away with me. I play the piano and sing. Music is good for the soul." I laughed. "And YouTube is my best friend. The tutorials for makeup and hairstyles you can find on that sucker blow my mind."

His eyes brightened with intrigue. "Wow, I'm impressed," he said, resting his chin in his hand. I watched as he lightly tapped his index finger against his cheek as if pondering me. His smile broadened, and he began to nod his head. "I knew there was a reason I liked you. I thought it was because you're stunningly beautiful, but now I see it is because I found a kindred spirit in you. A band member of the wannabe AC/DC band I'm thinking of starting."

I scoffed at his mockery, but a smile twisted at me. I was thoroughly enjoying myself in his company. He was an old soul like me.

As if we were on a speed date, he added more to my growing database of knowledge on him. "I do make a mean lasagna. I will make it for you sometime." He grinned, spreading his arms across the back of the booth.

Oh, I got him on this one. Smug bugger.

I arched a brow. "You're aware I'm half Italian, right?"

He faked a yawn. "I guessed. But still, I stand behind my lasagna," he said valiantly.

I tilted my nose and snorted. "Game on. My signature dish of butter sage gnudi would win hands down."

He threw back his head and laughed, his brown eyes bouncing with elation. "Are we competing now?"

"I'm simply stating the obvious. But yes, you got yourself a challenge," I affirmed, lifting my lips in delight.

"Do I sense a little bit of a fighter in you?" Amusement danced in his eyes.

"Maybe?" I smiled, peering down at my freshly painted robin blue nails.

He had a way of making me feel like I was wanted. I never dreamed friendship would come in the form of a guy—who happened to be the most gorgeous guy I had ever laid eyes on.

"Jewel?" Like the strumming of a harp, his voice called my name. He lowered his head to look up into my downturned eyes.

Lifting my gaze, I swept it over the five o'clock shadow darkening his strong jawline. "You okay?" he questioned, concern drawing at his brow line.

I nodded. "I was thinking about how nice it is to not be treated like a disease. As lame as that sounds, what I have wanted more than anything is a friend." I smiled sheepishly, but the softening of his eyes urged me to continue. "Someone who will be true to me and won't leave me behind. It's funny how something so small can become so daunting and damaging to your self-esteem."

He cocked his head as he looked at me but said nothing.

The insecurity lodged a growing lump in my throat. *Did I say too much? He thinks I am weird.* I rushed to explain myself. "What I want to say is thank you. Thank you for giving me a chance."

A perplexed gaze floated across his face. He watched me a moment without speaking.

*Don't sit there gawking at me. For the love of God, say something.*

Without a word, his hands slid across the table and gathered my hands. "I think I should be the one thanking you. You are more normal than most girls. There's no dramatics with you. You say it how it is, and I like that. I find it quite refreshing."

*Crisis averted.* I released a breath. "I'll take that as a compliment."

The warmth of his hands capturing mine sent tingles up my spine.

"Here we go," the waitress said, arriving with our food.

I jerked my hands back like I'd been caught doing something shameful.

Kaiden leaned back as the waitress set his rainbow rolls before him. Setting my cheeseburger and fries in front of me, she cocked me a wink and an approving smile. As she turned to walk away, she gave me a thumbs-up. Unbeknownst to him, thank God. I smiled politely at her insinuation of the prize she guessed was mine.

"What are your plans after graduation?" Kaiden asked,

pulling my attention back to him.

"My goal is to pursue a career as a vet. I've always had a passion for animals and have applied to a vet school in Calgary, Alberta."

He raised his eyebrows. "Wow, that's ambitious and awesome. Your grades must be up there to obtain the hope of getting into vet school." He whistled as he popped a few of my fries into his mouth.

"It's not like I have a social life or anything else to focus on but my grades and my future. In a way, it's been the one secure foundation I based my life on. Volunteering at the ranch fills the void of friendship." I was all too aware of how pathetic that made me sound. "I love those horses. Cherish, the horse I ride, was abused before she came to the ranch. No one could ride her. She has nasty scars from where her previous owner had spurred her. We learned to trust each other, and eventually, she allowed me to ride her. I like to think we helped heal each other in a way." Tears veiled my eyes, and my voice clogged with emotion. That horse had given me as much as I had given her. The ranch had become my second home, and without it, I didn't know where I'd be. The thought of it ruffled my sanity. Cherish had resurrected me from the dark grave which had once held me.

Later that night as I lay in bed, my phone alerted me of a text. Reaching for it on my nightstand, I read the four simple words he'd texted.

*I'll never leave you.*

I buried my face into my pillow, muffling my sobs. I cried for the years of hurt and loneliness stirring in me. I was falling for a guy who could not stop what had proven to be the inevitable. He would eventually leave … everyone always did.

# CHAPTER ELEVEN

*Jewel*

September cruised by, taking with it half of October. Kaiden, Finn, and I established a steadfast friendship. The hot guy, the loner, and the nerd. As time passed, our trio drew less open-mouthed gawking from passersby.

I never grew tired of peeking around my locker door to find Kaiden waiting. He often exaggerated his annoyances at my puttering with a huff and a sigh.

It was a Friday, the day of the bathroom incident. Right before my morning classes, nature summoned, so I made a quick pit stop before the bell rang. The bathroom split into two aisles of bold red stalls. My canvas shoes squeaked on the white tile as I ducked into the first stall. Locking the door, I hung my purse on the door hook.

The main door groaned open, and the clapping of heels on the tiles clipped my ears. Dread solidified my blood and my ears perked as Lexi's nasally voice parroted throughout the bathroom.

"Oh, my God. He is so damn hot. I could think of some fun things to do with that body of his. I can't for the life of me understand what he sees in that lame Jewel Hart."

I hustled to zip up my pants. Adrenaline vibrated through me, and fire sparks rocketed from my ears. I rotated around in the stall, contemplating what to do.

"Maybe she is good in the sack." Jess giggled. "She has to have something going for her as the guys seem to like her. Regardless of the fact she is a permanent resident of the loser bus. What does she expect after a year of being homeschooled? Did she think she wouldn't end up alone when she came back?"

I wanted to scream and cry all at the same time. Tears of frustration burned my eyes, begging for release.

*Stupid girls!* I seethed.

Why did they care so much about what I did? Why couldn't they bugger off and leave me the hell alone? Would it ever end?

Peering through the crack in the door, I surveyed the wolf pack.

Amy's voice cracked as she timidly spoke. "If you guys gave her half a chance, you would realize she isn't that bad."

Lexi and Jess swerve to pin her within their sights.

"Shut up, Amy! What do you know? You're lucky we allowed your pathetic self to be part of our group in the first place. Really, you should check yourself. Don't forget who made you." Lexi inched toward Amy dispensing her threat.

Amy crept backward. Jess—the muscle of the group, in both mouth and muscle mass—echoed Lexi's advancement toward Amy.

"Stop. Back off," Amy pleaded as she scurried to move out of their grasp.

"We'll stop as soon as you learn your place," Lexi warned.

"Yeah," Jess conceded.

I couldn't stand here hiding like a coward. I had to do something.

"This isn't going to end well," I whispered with a shake of my head before opening the stall door and walking out.

"All right, leave her alone." I addressed them while struggling to keep my voice from trembling. I folded my arms across my chest, concealing my shaky hands.

Lexi and Jess pivoted on their heels. Their eyes narrowed at my intrusion.

Fear quilted Amy's face. Her eyes warning me, she shook her head.

"Oh, look who it is. Eavesdropping are you, Hart?" Lexi clipped, her upper lip curling into a sneer.

Jess's eyes gleamed with delight as she circled me.

"You have a lot of nerve, Hart, to intrude on a conversation which doesn't involve you." Lexi's eyes flashed.

"Call me a fool, but I'm pretty sure my name came out of your lips. Any idiot could see this wasn't a conversation. But more along the lines of intimidation. Something you are a master of, Lexi." The shaking in my voice was undeniable.

"Remember who you are speaking to, slut." Jess's face turned lethal as she continued to make her rounds around me. She jammed the palm of her hand into my back.

*Breathe.* I rooted my feet to the ground. Nerves constricted my stomach, and my breakfast warned of its pending revolt.

Jess dragged her gel nail over the bare flesh of my arm

and tattooed her mark. I grimaced as the sting of her claw turned the skin red. My eyes raked over her as I moved out of her grasp.

*I will not break.*

"Does this make you feel powerful, Jessica? How about you, Lexi?" I replied grimly. "Do you get a thrill out of pouncing on people when they're outnumbered? You know as well as I do that you are sad, broken little girls. So you can drop the tough act because you are as weak as you consider me. The only difference between you and me is that I refuse to stay down in the gutter you have tried to place me in." A vibration moved through me as I made an effort to find my own strength.

Drained and longing to see the other side of the bathroom door, I shoved past a stunned Lexi. Only at the door did I halt. Turning to Amy, I said, "As for you, Amy. You have always been better than those two. It's time you realize it."

Amy raised a hand to her throat, her tea green eyes quivering.

I smiled at her. "You control your choices. Not these Chihuahuas." I glared at the dumbfounded pair.

I marched out of the bathroom, leaving the door swinging behind me.

Never had I felt so good.

I secured a table in the cafeteria. Kaiden texted this morning to inform me he wouldn't be at school today because he'd caught a flu bug. With Kaiden's absence from school, Finn and I would be flying solo.

Finn slammed his tray down, and the metal table echoed his displeasure. "Hey," he said.

I eyed the bridge of his glasses which appeared to be broken and taped back together.

I nudged a forkful of chicken Caesar salad at his glasses. "What happened there?" I scooped the fork into my mouth, waiting for him to explain.

"That jackass, Chad. That's what!" His crow black eyes snapped.

My eyebrows anchored.

"Oh, it gets better than that," he grumbled.

My blood sizzled at the nerve of the overstretched, muscled, baboon Chad Palmer.

Finn's body vibrated with rage as he reiterated what happened this morning. "In outdoor ed, we went canoeing. He intentionally sideswiped my canoe, sending my partner and me to the bottom of the germ-infested pond, which resulted in me having to get these from the office." He flicked at the light gray jogging pants and plain white t-shirt he wore.

"And the glasses? Did that happen then too?"

"No, it happened later in the guys' changing room. The outdoor ed teacher gave Chad detention for the next two days. He aimed to get even and voila. He is such a douchebag." Finn dropped his gaze to the apple he spun by the stem on the table. Misery and disheartenment gnawing at him.

The tightness in my chest deflated, and a wave of tenderness befell me. Reaching out, I gently squeezed his arm. "The thing to remember, Finn, is that we'll be getting out of here soon. When we've found our success in life. These people will still be stuck right here in the past, dealing with their wrongs.

They will never be able to shake it off. But we can, we have to." I aimed to encourage us both.

Finn smiled appreciatively as he twisted open his Sprite. "I've watched you for years—" he admitted as he raised his eyes to meet my gaze.

Catching sight of my visible frown, he protested, "Now, hold on a minute there, Miss Judgmental. It's not like that." He scowled at me before going on to defend his statement. "Like I started to say, I witnessed your struggles. I've been shoved into one too many lockers. As much as I thrive on knowledge to function, I would find excuses to stay home from school. The thought of coming here made me physically ill. My mind felt like it was drying up and becoming stupefied by the lack of education."

"You and me both, Finn. Pretty much every day, I go home with a migraine from the stress of school. I was in grade one, I think, when Mom started making sure to bring a plastic bag for me when she picked me up. The migraines were so bad, I'd vomit in her car on the way home."

He grimaced. "How do you stay positive?"

"What do you mean?"

"You don't lash out at people. You haven't become the bully. How do you keep grounded and sane?"

I had awoken in the twilight zone or hell had frozen over or whatever the terminology was that people said. I was sure of it. Was Finn Gracia seeking guidance from me? He was the overachiever and the smartest kid in school. But like me, he also was a target of bullying.

I shrugged, not quite sure how to respond to him.

An epidemic was spreading across our world and infecting us all. The rise in teen suicides because of it was astounding, and it weighed heavily on my mind.

"I've been in the low place they put me in far too long. Coming here has been a day-to-day struggle, and one I often don't want to wake up to. My parents have spent countless hours encouraging me and telling me I am amazing and all the stuff I believed parents are supposed to say. But I found the more I work on deleting the files of garbage stored in my subconscious, the more I started to believe in myself. I owe Kaiden and you a lot of credit for that. You are helping me see what my mom's been preaching for years. Besides, we can't let them win, now, can we?" I said with a grin.

He grinned, bobbing his head up and down.

"Can I sit here?" a girl's voice broke our conversation.

I glanced up to see Amy standing with her tray of lunch, eyeing me with uncertainty.

Finn and I glanced from her to each other, our mouths gaped open.

"All right?" I cocked a brow, taken aback by her request.

She sat down beside Finn, and he wiggled in discomfort at being in such close proximity to a beautiful girl.

In my opinion, Amy had a dream body. She tucked in, in all the right places. She could pull off a pair of jeans like no other girl in school. So what was the reason for her low self-esteem? Why had she allowed the likes of Lexi and Jess to dictate to her? I knew her to be a kid of the foster system until she was adopted by her parents when she was twelve. Had this fueled her actions?

Amy smiled at me. "I wanted to thank you for this morning."

I gave her a dismissive wave. "It was the right thing to do. After all, you got into that mess because you stood up for me.

So thank you," I cheered her courage.

She beamed at the positive reinforcement before her eyes hooded with a glare. "I hate those girls and myself. I don't want to be part of what they are anymore." Her luxurious auburn lashes brushed her cheeks as her head lowered.

Perplexed, I asked, "You've been friends for years. Why now?"

"Because of you. You gave me the courage I couldn't find in myself to break free. The odds were against you, but you stood up for what you believed. Those girls were steaming mad when you walked out of the bathroom with your nose turned up and owning your right to exist in this school. I may have wasted all these years trying to be their friend, but in all reality, I was bullied by them just as much as the next person. Those girls have knocked me down for too long. They made me feel worthless. Heck, I absorbed their belittling of me, and the little voice in my head agreed with them. If my own parents couldn't get clean from drugs to keep me, then I must not hold any value, right? I've spent my life wanting people to want me. I always knew my weakness stemmed from this, but I couldn't seem to rise above it. As for Jess, I believe she has an infatuation with Lexi that goes beyond what you would call normal. She admires everything about her and feeds off every word that comes out of her mouth."

She spoke her truth, and I respected her for it. A girl who hours ago was my enemy, now sat at my table confiding in me.

People had this misconception that bullying affects only the kids who were acne-covered and overweight with a mouth full of braces. When it affected us all—kids of all ages, shapes, sizes, and races. Pretty or not, we all became part of bullying at some point in our lives. Like the victims of bullying, the bullies themselves came in many forms.

Finn sat ogling Amy from his position at her side. He was love struck. His eyes gleamed with enchantment as he viewed the redhead beauty who sat with us. "Well, Amy, we would be more than happy to have you join our posse of coolness," Finn chorused.

I cringed as the words left his mouth. For his sake, I wanted to stuff them back in.

Oh, boy. Too many computer program adjustments for him. My gaze flickered from Finn to Amy, my teeth clenched as I waited for her reply.

Amy looked directly at him with a confidence rare for her. Finn melted under her gaze.

She reached out and adjusted his crooked glasses. "Thanks, Finn. I would like that a lot." Her face split into a gleeful grin, and to me, she said, "Thank you, Jewel, for accepting me. Even with our history."

"Trust is a powerful thing and a tough thing for me. But I'm willing to try. Baby steps is a good place to start. What do you say?" I smiled.

She flashed me a beautiful smile and gave a nod of her head.

Now, it was one hundred percent affirmed. I'd lost my mind. I made a pact with Amy, Lexi's right-hand sidekick. This year truly would be the turning point of my life.

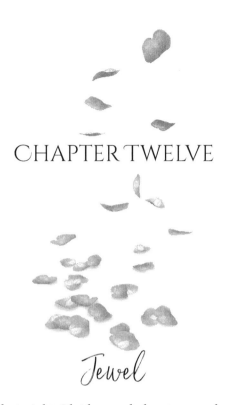

# CHAPTER TWELVE

*Jewel*

L ater that night, I laid sprawled out on my bed buried in
mountains of homework.

"How was school today?" Mom said, popping her
head into my room. Her figure was stunning in a red spandex
dress. For a woman pushing forty, she was still on point in the
fashion world. She stood twirling her timeless, genuine leather, five-inch black heels in her hands. Her brunette hair was
twisted into an elegant arrangement on the back of her head.
She was a walking commercial for ladies' office attire.

"Great actually," I said, nonchalantly.

A dumbfound expression crossed her face. "What,
really?"

"Yup, that's a fact."

"Oh, honey, it thrills me to hear you say that. What made
it great?"

I paused a moment too long, and in lightning speed,

Mom closed the distance between us. She sank down on my bed and gave my arm a gentle shake. "Child, if you don't tell me right now, I'm going to ground you for life." She swore an idle threat.

Sitting up and rocking my butt back to rest on my heels, I laughed. "Okay, take a breather."

"Easy enough for you to say." Her eyes narrowed, and her glossed lips set in a firm line.

Oh, no. The mom stare. I refrained from smirking.

For her sake, as she appeared to be developing a menopausal episode, I enlightened her. "Well, I think things are starting to look up for me. For one thing, I'm not feeling so alone anymore."

"I'm assuming you mean Kaiden?" Her mouth turned up into an all-too-happy smile.

"Yes, he is one reason. He appreciates me for me. At school, I'm growing accustomed to him waiting for me in the morning. Behind every door, I find him. His face lights up in happiness at the sight of me. I don't know. I guess it feels kind of nice to be wanted," I confided.

Mom's eyes danced with joy at my words. "I knew I liked that handsome young man. He is cute, and he's good to my girl. He is a keeper in this mama's books."

"We are only friends. Don't go getting ahead of yourself." I grinned. "But because of Finn and Kaiden, a social life isn't a dream anymore. It's something which now belongs to me." A smile tugged at my lips. I quickly filled her in on what happened in the bathroom today before adding, " I wanted to deck both of them right there. I envisioned all day about plunging their faces in the toilets and crowning them the porcelain goddesses they claim to be. But I refrained, so don't worry."

"It would have served them right." Mom laughed as the image played out in her mind.

"Oh, the thought of their faces is what got me through the first period with Mrs. Barker." I huffed. "Then, at lunch, Amy asked to join Finn and me at our table. She has sworn off those girls, and I believe her to be genuine."

Mom pressed her hands on either side of her face, and her olive complexion glowed with exhilaration at my news. Her shoulders began to rise and fall, and large teardrops dripped from her eyes.

Her tears caused my own tears, and I leaned forward, wrapping her in my arms. "I got this, Mom. I'll be okay."

"I know, sweet girl." Her voice muffled in my shoulder. We remained in each other's arms a little while longer before she pulled back. "Look at you, comforting me, when I'm the mom and the one who is supposed to comfort you. My tears are tears of joy. I promise. This happiness you have is all I've ever wanted for you. It's your right, and the one thing we could never give you." She sniffled and a small hiccup let loose from her.

I tilted my head sideways as I gazed at the woman who taken on my pain and carried it as if it was her own. She always told us kids that she and dad couldn't be our friends. That they had a duty to us, and it was to be the parents. Their job was to set guidelines for us to follow. 'Too many parents try to be friends,' she'd said more than once. It was comical to me as she'd been the only friend I'd ever had until now.

From my bedroom window, I realized night had fallen. In need of fresh air and a change of scenery, I waddled down to the kitchen in my faux-fur slipper booties. A lover of all things warm and cozy, I'd swaddled my body in my favorite teal fleece pjs.

Tonight, you could feel the chill in the air. The red maples out front had begun to shed their leaves as the night temperature started to drop.

I made a cup of mint hot chocolate, topping it with a mountain of whip cream and two extra pinches of chocolate flakes. Retrieving the charcoal-gray knitted blanket placed over the arm of the couch in the main living room, I scooped it around my shoulders and shuffled out the French doors to the backyard.

I stepped out on the stone patio which expanded and embraced our outdoor living room. A brilliant glow of fire came from the fire pit. Miles lounged in one of the vibrant yellow cushioned chairs. Scuffing my slipper-covered feet toward him, I sat down on the couch beside him.

He looked up at my approach. "Hey, Jewel," he said before turning his eyes back to the captivating inferno in front of him.

"Hey, Miles. Hope you don't care if I join you."

"I guess I don't have a choice since you planted your butt on that couch, now, do I?" he joked with a smile which danced in his eyes but avoided his mouth.

"No, you don't," I said, crinkling up my nose and sticking out my tongue. "What were you thinking of before I blew up your world with my presence?" I layered my words with sarcasm.

He half-shrugged, banning me from his previous

thoughts. Miles was a loner by his own choice. He was calm, cool, and collected on the outside, but I believed him to be a thinker. Maybe even more sensitive than he let on.

"Christmas is just around the corner. What are you thinking of getting Mom and Dad?" I asked, placing my hot chocolate to my lips. The sweet, pure goodness made my taste buds yelp in delight.

Could've handled an extra shot of chocolate syrup.

Twisting his black cap backward as he leaned forward to rest his elbows on his knees, he gazed at the fire. As a man of few words, he said, "No idea yet."

"Typical guy," I grumbled at him. "Waiting for the last moment."

He snorted. "Maybe us guys put more thought into our gifts and don't hurry to check the task off our list," he jabbed, removing his hat, and swiped a hand through his hair before replacing it.

I chuckled. "Is that your theory?"

"Something like that," he said.

"Meet any girls at university? Like one, I suppose, you could hitch up with. I mean you're twenty, and we've yet to see a girl enter this house." I nudged my head toward the house.

"What's the hurry? Why tie myself down with a girl when I have other priorities? Like finish school. Also, I booked a ticket for Japan after next semester." He glanced at me, waiting for my reaction.

He had a love for all things Japanese and was a faithful student, spending multiple nights a week in a ninjutsu class.

"Do Mom and Dad know?"

Mom was going to freak. Straight up lose her noodles. Though she supported Miles's desire to go to Japan, we would need to peel her claws from him. It was a standing joke between Dad and me over the love she bore for her first born.

"No, but I will. I need to figure out how to break it to her. Well, to both of them, actually."

"I suggest sooner than later." I added my sisterly advice.

"You're right." He removed his hat and sat back, stretching his long legs out in front of him and crossing his ankles.

I sensed there was deeper concern occupying my brother's mind. "You're nervous about venturing out on your own, aren't you?" I said.

Once again, he was silent, and the cracking sound of the fire filled our silence. Tiny sparks jolted out of the pit and floated up into the evening sky. I followed a few with my eyes, waiting for him to speak.

Time ticked by. We were obviously following Miles's timeline. Everything he did was done at a slow agonizing pace. An hour for a shower, an hour to go to the bathroom. An hour to eat breakfast. An hour to load the dishwasher—

"Well," he retrieved his tongue and dignified me with an answer.

About flipping time. God almighty.

"I guess a part of me is. Mom and Dad have managed to give us it all. Love, security, guidance, and the desire to explore the world, but the world is different when you can't stand behind their protection anymore." He peered down at his hat as he twisted it anxiously in his hands.

"I hear you. Maybe that's when we rely on the knowledge and leadership they've instilled in us."

He chuckled lightly as he shuffled his size ten sneakers on the ground in front of him. "Oh, so now you're the book of wisdom, are you?" he teased.

"Lately, I've found more purpose to enjoy my life."

"That wouldn't have anything to do with 'dreamy eyes' would it?" He made kissing faces in the air with his hat as his imaginary partner.

Heat ignited in my cheeks, "Oh, please. It's not like you ever kissed a girl."

He shrugged his shoulders unaffected, "Wouldn't you like to know?"

"Seriously?" I broke into an ear to ear grin.

"Maybe." He smiled.

Knowing my brother to be the tormentor he was, that would be the last word I'd get on that topic. He stood to go, but before walking away, he turned and said, "I'm glad to see it, Jewel. You are worth everything we believe you are and much more."

Tears stung my eyes as I gazed up at the brother I had always looked up to and admired. As a child, I had hung on his every word. He had been my hero. "Thanks, Miles."

He sauntered toward the house without another word.

# CHAPTER THIRTEEN

*Jewel*

W eeks had passed since the bathroom incident. Amy stuck to her new path in life and left Lexi and Jess behind. She was proving to be the girl I often thought she could be. Our friendship developed, and with that, she became a part of our team of misfits.

"Where's Amy, by the way?" I asked Finn and Kaiden as we entered the school.

"I haven't seen her yet today," Finn replied before heading off toward his locker.

With a bemused smile, I considered the light skip in Finn's step. "Is it me, or is Finn dressing a little different lately?"

"I hadn't noticed. I've been a little preoccupied myself," Kaiden answered, his shoulders hunching as he shoved his hands in his pockets.

I shot him a side glance, puzzled by his comment, but

said nothing. He leaned against the locker adjacent to mine as I tossed my stuff inside. Retrieving the books I needed for my first class, I closed my locker and turned to him.

"I think Finn is madly engrossed in Amy. I'm not sure about her feelings for him, but I hope he doesn't end up hurt."

Kaiden grew serious as he pondered my words. "Now that you mention it, he has been extra happy. I don't pay attention to what he wears, but he has been kind of giddy."

My eyes narrowed at him. "You're too busy pretending to flirt with me to notice much of anything else. Good thing I know you're teasing—"

"How—"

"I'm going to go find Amy. I'll see you at lunch?" I yelled over my shoulder as I hustled down the hall in the direction of her locker.

"Jewel!" he called after me. "My God, I swear I don't know what to do with you."

I waved a hand, dismissing his pleas as I rounded the corner to another hall of lockers. Unfortunately for Amy, she had to keep the locker she signed up for at the first of the year, meaning Lexi and Jess were in her path of morning traffic every day.

Amy stood at her locker. The door was open, but her jean-clad legs appeared below. As I drew near, the sound of her sniffle reached me.

"Hey Amy, you coming down with a cold?" I opened her locker wider. After one look at her face, it became obvious a cold wasn't the reason for her case of the sniffles. Her eyes were puffy and red from crying. Black streaks of mascara ran a course over her cheeks. "Amy? What's wrong?"

"Nothing." She fumbled mindlessly around in her locker.

"Bull! Something is wrong, and I bet in one guess I could pinpoint who is the cause of all this," I released a raspy breath.

"Well … I …" she stammered.

"Classes will be starting soon. We need to go wash your face, and you can fill me in on what happened. Got it?" I placed my hand on my hip.

A smidgen of a smile slipped from her lips. She nodded.

In the bathroom, she removed a folded piece of paper from inside her textbook.

"Here, read this." She pressed the paper into my hand. She ripped off a piece of paper towel and dampened it and blotted her face.

I opened the folded paper.

*Bitch, you'd better watch your back. I wouldn't be found anywhere alone, or you will get what you deserve.*

My pulse skyrocketed, and my cheek twitched as I looked from the note to her.

"Is it from Lexi?" I asked, already knowing the answer.

"Of course, it's from Lexi. It's her handwriting." Her eyes glared at me from the mirror.

"Well, we can't let her get away with it."

"What exactly do you propose we do Jewel?" she said sharply. "Who are we going to tell? Our parents? Like I want people knowing I told my parents and they had to come to my rescue. Over my dead body will I be doing that. That will only add to it."

"You need to report this to the principal, or maybe it's best to go to Mr. B first. He made an effort when Lexi smashed my head into the locker. Never changed her any, but she did get suspended for a few days. We need to tell someone who will do something about this, Amy. Lexi and Jess need to pay for their actions. Nothing will ever change if we keep it quiet."

"Maybe. We'll see." She tossed the paper towel in the garbage. "We'd better get to class."

"All right. But promise you'll tell someone."

She huffed, and we left the bathroom.

"For you, I will. But I guarantee you it will be of no use."

"That's all I ask," I said as we walked toward our classroom.

"Thanks for caring."

"Of course, isn't that what friends are for? We both know I'm not an expert on the friend thing, but I'm trying to be the best friend I can be."

"For what it's worth, in a few short weeks, you've become the best one I've ever had," she said with a smile.

We were on the tail end of the students to enter English class.

"Hurry it along, girls." Mrs. Barker's voice made me cringe.

"Hey, Mrs. Barker, can I speak to you?" I heard Amy say from behind me.

My heart plunged and my feet froze.

No Amy, not her. What was she thinking? Clearly, she isn't thinking. There was no way. The note must have unsettled her more than even I knew.

"What is it, Amy?" Mrs. Barker said.

I wish I hadn't, but I swerved to look at them.

"No Amy, not her," I squeaked.

Mrs. Barker arched a brow, and her mouth twisted. "Excuse me, Jewel. Can I help you?"

"No. I was talking to Amy."

"I believe Amy was speaking to me. So I suggest you

mind your own affairs and take a seat."

I glanced quickly at Amy and shook my head.

"Okay," I said, leveling my eyes on Mrs. Barker's.

"In this century, Jewel." Irritation exuded from every hair on her body.

I locked my jaw and held my tongue and went to sit in the first empty seat I came to. My eyes turned back to Amy and Mrs. Barker.

"All right, Amy. What is it?"

"Never mind. It's nothing."

"Well, it certainly isn't nothing if you brought it up. Now speak up and get on with it so I can start my class."

Amy spoke quietly as she held out the note for Mrs. Barker to view. My eyes darted from them to Lexi who sat in her usual seat with a satisfied smug look on her evil face.

"I suggest you get over it." My eyes flashed back at Amy as Mrs. Barker's words hit me. Mrs. Barker crumpled up the note and chucked it in the trash.

Amy's face mottled and her eyes pained, she slowly walked down the aisle toward a seat, forcing her to pass by Lexi. As she walked by, Lexi dropped her backpack on the floor by her desk. Amy stumbled but caught herself.

"Oops, better watch where you are going," Lexi said with a sweet demon possessed smile.

Amy continued on to the seat and plopped down. She folded her hands on the desk and never looked up. My eyes burned into the side of her head, demanding she looks at me. When she did, there were no tears; anger replaced her disheartenment. I smiled, reminding her I cared before returning my eyes back to the despicable teacher I had the honor of listening to for the next hour and a half.

## Kaiden

It was Friday, and the end of the school day couldn't come fast enough. I longed for the weekends from the moment I walked into first period Monday mornings. The faster I could kiss school goodbye, the better. But today I wouldn't be getting out of here so fast. My social studies teacher was allowing me to stay after school to finish an essay I forgot was due. The words on the page blurred as my mind began to wander to the future. Where would life take me?

So many times in the past few years, I had considered dropping out of school to get a full-time job. Maybe if I had, we would still be in our own home. It was a damned if you did, damned if you didn't situation. We needed the money. But if I'd quit, my life would never amount to anything. I wanted to make my own way in life, but it grew more daunting as graduation drew near. Mom was getting better … well, for the time being anyway. She wanted me to make something of myself as much as I wanted to. The thoughts of going off to university and leaving her behind scared the life out of me. What would happen to her?

Then, there was Jewel. Where was this friendship—as she liked to call it—taking us? I was determined to make her my girlfriend. But when I showed her I was interested in her, she brushed me off. With her going off to vet school, did this mean she didn't see a future for us? Maybe this had been for nothing? I didn't want a senior year fling. I needed something of substance and security in my life.

When I texted her about going to High Park this weekend and she texted back *Sure* with a smiley face and nothing more, my heart sank to my knees. Maybe friendship was all she wanted. Maybe I'd been wrong about her returning my feelings. Whatever it was, I wanted to know where I stood in her life. If she put me in the friend zone, then I would settle for that. Life now without her somehow seemed to hold no purpose. Losing her made me feel like my heart would shrivel up and stop beating.

"Kaiden, are you about done?" The social studies teacher's voice vibrated through the la la land in my head.

"Yes, sir," I replied and scribbled down my last sentence. Grabbing my backpack, I dropped the essay into his collection tray and hurried out the door.

At my car, I dumped my textbooks into the back seat. The parking lot was vacant except for Chad's car and a sophomore kid leaning over the driver's side window. The driver handed the kid something that he quickly put in his pocket. You would have to be a dummy not to realize a drug deal just went down. The kid jumped on his skateboard and skated toward me. I eyed him as he passed me.

He nodded his mousey brown dreadlocks at me as he skated past. "Hey," he said.

I raised my eyebrows. Ballsy. With a shake of my head, I glanced toward Chad's car as it rolled slowly past me. Chad sat behind the steering wheel grinning smugly. He shot me a cocky wave before he peeled out.

This guy had no shame. Driving by in his fancy car acting like selling drugs to that kid was no different than hitting a drive-thru. Creeps like him peeved me off. No matter how much money he had, it would never be enough. If you swiped his ass crack with a debit card, money would shoot out. Some people could have it all but still thirst for more.

As I drove home, the sour taste of Chad's misdeeds lingered. Maybe because prescription drugs had stolen years of my mother's life from me. Watching my mother detox when she tried to get off them was chiseled into my memory. Chad didn't care how many lives he ruined, and this fueled my growing dislike for him. How many kids would Chad destroy by leading them down the deadly road of drugs?

# CHAPTER FOURTEEN

*Jewel*

Saturday morning, I still lay in bed gazing aimlessly at the ceiling when Kaiden texted he was on his way. I kicked the blankets back and flew around my room in a panic to get ready.

There was no time to put on a face. "It will be an all-natural day today," I said to my reflection in the mirror. Which was fine with me. It was too much of a bother to wash the stuff off. Too many times, I'd gone to bed with makeup on only to awake to find one more zit to add to my collection … sigh. Besides, the few extra minutes of sleep were worth the sacrifice. It wasn't like Kaiden hadn't seen my naked face before.

I jumped up and down, wiggling my thighs in my "feel good" jeans. Oh, for God's sake. I sucked in my breath and held it as I fought to pull the zipper up. My struggle was real as I pinched my finger in the buttonhole to try to get the darn jeans done up. There. I whispered in relief and blew out the air constricting my lungs. Ugh … I glanced in the mirror. Though they looked great on me, there was no way I was going to enjoy an hour ride to and from the park sandwiched in these things.

*You've got to lay off the fast food.*

Downstairs, I tugged on my red knitted mittens and pushed my matching hat snugly down over my head. Zipping up my crisp white jacket, I stepped out on the front step.

Holy, Hannah. The frozen ground under my navy-blue sneakers snarled back at me. I second-guessed my choice at forgoing my Uggs, but Kaiden pulled into the drive as I considered going back in to get them.

I waved a mitten hand. He smiled as he bounced out of the car.

"You couldn't wait a minute longer to catch a peek at me," he said with a smirk.

"Sure, that's exactly what it is. I paced the floor in anticipation of your arrival. Oh, Kaiden, come to me, my prince." I put a hand to my heart to portray a damsel in distress.

"Fair enough. A woman who knows what she wants. I'm digging it," he said, a grin capturing him as he hurried to open my door.

I squinted my eyes into slits before I broke a smile.

Saturday morning traffic was at a minimum on the highway, and we made good timing getting to the park. Kaiden pulled into the parking lot and took the first available spot. Killing the engine, he turned to me. "You ready?"

I nodded, eager to be out of his cramped car.

"Come on, let's go," he said as he opened his door. Ducking his head, he swung his long, muscular frame out. I sat for a brief second, admiring his physique as he stood and stretched.

He bent his head back inside the car. "Beauty, you coming?" he asked, reaching for our cafe lattes in the cup holder.

"Right, yes," I said and hustled out of the car.

The click of the door locks sounded followed by the beep of his alarm. I looked over the roof of the car and met his eyes. Surely, it must be a crime to be that good looking. He smiled back at me.

I zipped my jacket up under my chin, and we began to walk toward the nearest trail. The park wasn't overly busy, but the activity was constant. A jogger whipped by us with his giant headphones on and beads of excursion bubbling on his forehead. His spandex shorts and tank top left his exposed skin red from its exposure to the elements. I shivered at the sight of him as he ran by and tucked my chin farther down into my down-filled jacket. Kaiden took my shiver for me being cold and slipped his arm around my shoulders, pulling me into the curve of his arm. The goose bumps already pricking at me multiplied and radiated across my body.

Birds chirped from their perches on the trees. In areas, the tops of the trees had begun to curve over the walking trail. The sun was bright and blinding against the clear blue skies. Tree limbs hung low from last night's snowfall. A squirrel scurried across the trail in front of us. The perfect morning for a walk. A walk you saw lovers in a romantic movie take.

Raising my latte to my lips, I sipped while gazing at the beauty of the nature around us.

"Beautiful here, isn't it?" Kaiden smile was infectious. Removing his arm from my shoulder, he slid his hand into mine.

"When was the last time you came here?"

"When I was fifteen." His eyes turned to stare at the trees to his left.

"So before your dad?"

"Yes, Mom never wanted to come back. My mom has suffered from extreme depression since his passing. The past three years have been difficult. One day, I think I'm getting past it. But other days, like today and being in this place, it's like yesterday all over again. After his death, my mom, I …" He coughed, clearing his throat.

I tightened my hand in his.

"I came home one day, and my mom had …well, she tried to take her own life."

"What?" My words came out as a cry, and my footsteps stopped. "Kai, I'm so sorry."

He shrugged his shoulders like he was okay, yet he could not hide the ache in his eyes.

"She was hospitalized and put on suicide watch. It was the worst period of my life so far. I thought losing Dad was hard, but this was so much worse."

"How is she now?" I asked with concern.

"She has her days. She used to hold down a successful job. Mom put a lot of time into charities and foundations. She used to be so ambitious, but that all went up in smoke. We were falling behind on our bills and our family home went into foreclosure. This summer, we moved in with my grandparents. Then I met you, and the rest is history." He exhaled a deep breath, and his body relaxed.

He looked at my mitten-covered hand encased in his. Unclasping our hands, he removed my mitten and entwined his fingers between mine, and a content smile tugged at the corners of his lips.

"No words can describe how grateful I am to my grandparents. Now with their help, they have given me more time to pursue the things I want. Like you." The playful and sometimes troubled Kaiden stepped aside and a more serious Kaiden took his place.

"Come sit with me." He led me to a wooden bench off to the side of the trail. Using a gloved hand, he wiped the snow from the bench.

Once we were seated, my eyes searched his face. His body language made it clear he was nervous. He wanted to say something but appeared to be wrestling with himself on how to say it. My brain started to take me down the path of self-doubt. I worried I might have done something wrong, but then I gritted my teeth in annoyance. He wasn't like that.

He reached out and replaced the mitten on my ice-cold hand. Taking both my hands in his, he gazed into my eyes. A band of drummers beat in my chest as my nerves spiked. His eyes were gentle as they continued their piercing autopsy. I paused for a second with sudden understanding. Wait a minute. Was this what I thought it was?

"Jewel, I've wanted to say this for a long time. I think you are amazing. Never has a girl had the effect on me like you've had. Something about you makes me know I need you in my life. Your beauty radiates from the inside. What makes you so much more beautiful is you don't even know how beautiful you are. From that day in the coffee shop, I knew I had to know more about you. The first day of school I spotted you, and it was like fate was saying 'go get her.' So who am I to deny fate?" He clasped a hand over his heart.

I was aware of my hanging jaw, so I snapped it closed. All

words abandoned me.

He liked me. He really liked me. The ballerina in my stomach danced her debut.

Suddenly, I'm floating on a cloud, peering down at the young couple sitting on a bench on a winter day. Their hands were interlocked and …

"Jewel, I really like you." He recaptured my drifting mind and stole my words and made them his own. "Like I have never liked a girl before. What I want to say is that I want to spend this year and much more together."

"Together?" I said. I needed him to say it straight.

He laughed. Dropping his eyes, he began to scuff his sneakers on the snow-covered ground. "You are going to make this difficult, aren't you?" he mused with a shake of his head. Lifting his eyes to hold my gaze, he asked, "Jewel Hart, will you be my girlfriend?"

For real? My body felt like it had been pricked with tiny needles. It made me feel alive.

*Please don't wake me from this dream.* He picked me. Of all the girls Kaiden could've had, he wanted me.

"I … umm, " I looked away, searching for a proper reply. He touched the side of my cheek and turned my eyes back to him.

The always confident Kaiden cracked under my hesitation. "Jewel, you do share the same feelings, right?"

"No, I mean, yes, I do. I'm scared. You are too good to be true. I'm afraid to let myself fully care only for you to abandon me."

"Jewel, I am not the others. I will not leave you. I promise you this." He stroked the curve of my cheekbone. A fire of emotion and desire to be in his arms surged through me.

I began to tremble, and Kaiden sensed my worry, pulling me into his embrace. I laid my cheek against his chest. The pounding of his heart matched the beat of mine. In his arms, I felt safe.

Could I trust him with my heart? I had to. I couldn't not explore where a relationship with him would take me. Had he proven to be a guy worth fighting for with his dedication to helping his mom?

Yes, Kaiden Carter was a guy worth the risk.

"Yes," I mumbled into the amazingness of his chest.

I swear, I heard his heart stop. He pulled me back and viewed me at arm's length. Happiness formed a halo around him.

"You know you can't take back that yes, or my heart will forever be broken into shards of discarded glass," he warned, his eyes skipping with mirth.

"I said yes," I said with a giggle.

His eyes outlined my lips. Somersaults demanded control of my stomach as he lowered his head and our lips touched. I welcomed his soft kiss, and there, under the perfect winter day, we sealed our relationship with my first kiss.

# CHAPTER FIFTEEN

*Jewel*

D ecember trickled in, bringing with it endless snow-storms. My eighteenth birthday was days away. Always one for a good party, Mom had set the plans in motion. She arranged a skating party at the local outdoor rink. Kaiden's grandparents and mom were invited.

My thoughts whirled as we drove to the rink. Only days had passed since Kaiden asked me to be his girlfriend, and this would be my first time meeting his family. An inner restlessness consumed me. Would they like me? Would they think I was good enough for him? Mom never thought any-one was good enough for her precious Miles. Would his mom feel the same?

Alas, we parked in the parking lot of the arena, and ev-eryone piled out. Dad popped the trunk, and he and Miles unloaded blankets, skates, and a helmet for Ellie. I shut the raised door to the SUV as a black Town Car pulled into the parking lot. The hired driver stepped out and circled the car to open the door for his passengers.

A pleasant, smiling lady who appeared to be in her forties stepped out first. She looked at my family and waved eagerly. The tension building all morning subsided a little. An older man with silver feathered back hair nodded a thank you to the driver and turned to help the final passenger. Kaiden's grandma, an older vision of his mom, came into view.

Kaiden's grandpa pulled a blue toque from the inside pocket of his gray wool winter trench coat and yanked it down over his neatly combed hair. Seeing our approach, he grinned a radiant smile at us. My dad stepped forward and offered his hand in a handshake. Multiple introductions went around, and Kaiden took my hand and led me to his mom.

"Mom, I'd like you to meet Jewel," he beamed with pride as he introduced me.

"Jewel, it's a pleasure. I've been dying to meet the girl who stole my son's eye." Her olive green eyes twinkled with satisfaction as she observed me.

"Nice to meet you, Mrs. Carter." I flashed a smile.

"Kaiden has told me a lot of wonderful things about you." She smiled with a fondness for someone she'd never met. My heart warmed that Kaiden had painted a positive image of me in her head.

"Well, I think he is pretty special too. Though he tends to get a thrill out of tormenting me. I already have two guys in my life who do that religiously." I jutted my head toward Miles and Dad while a smile played at my mouth.

"Yes, that is my Kaiden. Full of funnies and jabs. As mischievous as he is, he is a good son. The best a mother could hope for," she said, beaming at Kaiden. I couldn't help but notice that behind her smile lay a weariness.

"You two can stop all the chirping about my greatness. Even I get embarrassed." His eyes gleamed as he dangled an arm around his mom's shoulder.

My heart ruptured into pieces. How many times had I been told, "Watch how a man treats his mom because that is how he will treat you." I turned to look at Mom and found her observing the exchange. As our eyes met, a glimmer of tears lined her eyes. She smiled and nodded her head. Her actions said it all. She had been right, and a smile expanded across my face. I hated when she would say something and then not long after turn out to be right. But at this moment, I was more than willing to let her be.

## Kaiden

Later, the adults sat drinking hot chocolate on the benches to the side of the rink. They were caught up in idle chitchat. Mom sat engaged in what appeared to be a cheerful conversation with Mrs. Hart. She leaned forward, laughing at something Jewel's mom had said. I smiled at the lightheartedness that passed between them.

Finn and Miles did laps around Amy and Jewel. Like hockey had been a frequent winter sport for them. I chuckled as I watched Amy and Jewel. For Canadian girls, it was apparent skating wasn't a regular activity for them as they resembled freshly born foals who couldn't quite figure out their legs.

Turning, I noticed Ellie grasping the side of the rink wall as she inched her way to us. Her skates were replaced with boots. I kicked back the blades of my skate and swished across the ice to retrieve her.

"Hello, Miss, may I have this skate dance." Putting a gloved hand to my chest, I gave her a slight bow.

Ellie grinned ear to ear and offered her tiny, white mitten hand.

"Kai, you're silly, but I like you." She illuminated. The nipping wind dusted her rosy cheeks with frost. Her feet started to slip, and I steadied her.

"How about we share my skates?" I suggested.

Her button nose wrinkled up, and her eyebrows dipped down in her confusion. "What do you mean?"

"Like this." I picked her up and placed her feet on the front of my skates.

"Oh," she said with a giggle of excitement.

"Jules, look at me," Ellie called out, a glow covering her sweet face as we sailed around the rink.

"Ellie appears to be the better skater of the Hart sisters," I shouted out.

"Should I be concerned that your skate dancing with a younger version of me?" Jewel said with a laugh as we came alongside her and Amy.

"Maybe. She is pretty cute," I tossed back and leaned down to plant a quick kiss on her lips.

"Jules, this is my special time. Go skate with Miles," Ellie said, claiming me as her prize.

"But Ellie, Kai is my boyfriend," Jewel reminded her.

"But you have him all to yourself, all the time," she complained.

Miles glided in beside us on an angle, shooting ice dust as his skates bladed the ice. "Ellie, I'm disappointed in you." A straight-faced Miles looked down at his little sister.

"What? Why?" Ellie's eyes shone with worry as she gazed up at her brother.

"I thought I was your favorite guy? Then Kaiden comes along and you throw me out like yesterday's trash."

Ellie appeared disturbed as she looked from me to Miles. She rolled his words over in her head. "Miles, you are my brother. We can't get married. Jules says so. I can like you, but you can't be my boyfriend," she stated innocently.

"So you are keeping your options open?" Miles asked, stifling a grin.

Clearly, his words confused Ellie, so he dropped his teasing.

"Never mind, kiddo." He gave her cheek a light squeeze and offered his hands to her. "Want to give my feet a spin?"

Her face lit up at the opportunity to spend time with Miles. A bubbling Ellie readily took his hands, and like a fairy perched on a lily pad, she floated off.

I looped an arm around the vision of blond in front of me. "Now, I have the birthday girl all to myself."

Amy cleared her throat loudly. "Technically, I'm right here, but I received the hint. Loud and clear." Amy laughed before darting off to meet Finn on the opposite end of the ice.

I looked down into Jewel's eyes. I hadn't seen eyes quite like hers before, ones that changed with her mood. Now, they gleamed tensely up at me. Her irises were currently the color of a blue jay as happiness fluttered in them. I twirled her around to rest her back against my chest. I placed my hands on her hips, and we glided effortlessly around the ice as if we were skating on air.

It was no secret I had fallen victim to the beautiful immortal I held in my hands.

# CHAPTER SIXTEEN

*Jewel*

All semester, walking into English class unraveled my nerves. Something about Mrs. Barker put me on high alert. She didn't like me, I was certain of it. I saw it in the eagle-eyed glare she cast on me. In a way, her body posture grew a few inches when she came near me.

Today would prove to be no different. She was in a mood, and it was apparent as soon as she walked in the room. The reverberation of her books on her desk zapped all positivity from us. We sat up straight, and all eyes fastened on her. In a constricted voice, she let us know what she required of us for this class. She quickly broke us up into groups. It didn't surprise me when she placed Amy, Lexi, and I together along with another guy. Intentional on Mrs. Barker's part? I had my suspicions.

Minutes later, the students froze as her voice cut through the room.

"Scott, you will never go anywhere or be anyone." She flared with impatience at a student who struggled with a learning disability.

I bristled at her demeaning him, but I couldn't breathe a word. I willed myself to focus on our project and tune everything else out. Our group stood huddled together in a corner at the back of the classroom. After several minutes of Lexi talking about herself and anything but the project at hand, I spoke up and tried to take charge.

"We need to select a leader to present our project to the class tomorrow. Any volunteers?" I looked around my group.

Lexi opted out as she raised a hand to inspect her nails with disinterest.

"I will," Amy said with slight hesitation.

Lexi scoffed and dropped her hand. "Why would we let you take control and speak for us? We will fail for sure. You are such a loser, Amy. Your parents didn't want you, and we certainly don't." Lexi bared her teeth but kept her voice to a whisper.

My alarm to her cruel words elevated my voice. "Lexi, how dare you!"

The words barely escaped me before I felt her talons dig into my shoulders from behind. I was caught off guard as she spun me around.

Face to face with Mrs. Barker, fear devoured me, and I began to tremble under her glare. Her green eyes narrowed into slits, her red stained lips curled into an ugly snarl. "You, Jewel, are a thorn in my side and a distraction to this class." She pointed her finger in my face. "I should send you straight to the principal's office for your behavior. You will no longer be part of this group project. You will complete it on your own. Move your butt to that desk. Understood?"

"But … Mrs. Barker, you misunderstood," Amy said.

"Can it, Amy. I don't want to hear it," she said with a sneer.

Amy dropped her head and wrapped her arms tightly around herself.

Moving to the desk as instructed, I rolled over Mrs. Barker's lash-out in my head. I understand my raised voice had distracted the class. But her pent-up dislike for me left me demoralized and confused.

My body burned with humiliation. Alienated from my group, I dared to peek back in their direction. Mrs. Barker had moved Lexi to the side and was talking softly to her. I watched her cast a doting smile at Lexi, offering her comfort with a light rub of her arm. The two glanced in my direction briefly before turning back to their exchange of words. It was obvious who their conversation was about. The injustice of it all boiled my blood.

*This was absolute bull crap!* I seethed.

Later that night, I sought out Mom in hopes she could help me sort through the turmoil which had pummeled me all day since English class. My bare feet echoed across the travertine tiles to the aroma of sautéing garlic and onions drifting from the kitchen.

Mom glanced up from chopping vegetables when I entered. Her tired face from an early start at the office brightened at the sight of me. "Hey Jewel, exactly the face I wanted to see.

Can you chop these veggies while I get the meat going?"

"Yup." I retrieved the knife she offered.

The chicken sizzled as she dropped it into the hot frying pan.

I waited for her everyday questions.

"How was school?"

As expected, there it was.

"Overall, it was good. But," I started to say, and I didn't miss her suck in a breath at the word but. "You know how I've been trying to deal with school-related issues on my own?"

"Yes," she drew out her reply.

From my chopping station at the island, I glanced at her. Her body became rigid as she waited for me to continue.

"Well, today something happened, and I'm not sure how to deal with it."

"Okay?" she said, her back remained turned to me as she cranked her neck side to side to relieve her building tension.

I quickly reiterated what had happened in English class. Her eyes charred with anger as she turned from the stove and started pacing the kitchen floor. She rubbed her temples with two fingers.

"Okay, I will deal with this," she finally said.

Dad peeked around the corner with his briefcase in hand. "Hello, my favorite girls. What's going on in here?"

Mom swiveled to face him, and his steel blue eyes inspected the firm hold of her jaw.

"What's wrong?" he asked, his puzzlement circulating from her to me.

"I need to talk to you in the office," Mom said hotly. She was wound up. Adrenaline seeped from the tips of her toes as she marched from the room.

"Uh, okay?" His gaze clouded, and he looked at me before following her.

I crept down the hall after them. Mom's raised voice filtered out from behind the slightly opened door of the office. She gave Dad the full brunt of the anger blistering in her.

"It's not right, Quinn. The child has gone through enough. This isn't the first time a teacher has treated her like this. You know as much as I do how teachers like Mrs. Barker can affect a student. We both have experienced it ourselves. Jewel's peers bullying her is bad enough but teachers too?" She broke into Italian, which was a common habit of hers when she couldn't articulate what she was feeling in English. She always seemed angrier when she spoke in her native tongue.

"I have half a mind to go down there and rip a strip off Mrs. Barker." She reverted back to English.

"Well, we can't let it slide." I heard Dad assure her.

"I can't stand it, Quinn. I want people to leave her alone. All these nasty girls at her all the time. The school system needs to be aware of these teachers and weed them out. Teachers like that are helping to raise our youth. It's a complete and utter joke." Mom's voice cracked, and she began to sob.

Their voices became hushed whispers, and guilt ate at me. I'd caused her this pain. What was it about me that made life hard for everyone? Back in the kitchen as I lifted the knife to continue chopping the vegetables, my salty tears spilled down my cheeks. The knife in my hand grew blurred in my fountain of tears, and the vegetables on the cutting board disappeared altogether.

"Jules?" Ellie's small voice cut through my tears. I glanced down to find her standing beside me, her blue eyes round with concern.

I stared at her blankly.

"What's wrong, Jules?" She outlined my face with her eyes in search of an answer. "Did those kids be mean to you again?" Her mouth stiffened in protectiveness.

I ruffled her downy curls. "Don't worry your little head about Sissy's troubles, okay?" I forced a bright smile as I quickly wiped the tears away. I reached down and lifted her into my arms. She wrapped her arms around my neck and patted my back.

"I don't want them kids hurting you, Jules," her tiny voice murmured in my ear.

"I know, Ellie. I love you." I squished her tightly. Her sweetness and love were like soothing ointment placed on a gaping wound. I whispered a wish into the universe that she would not face the struggles in school I had.

# CHAPTER SEVENTEEN

*Jewel*

Two days later, I woke with a killer migraine. Immediately, my stomach churned with the fret and worry of facing Mrs. Barker. Yesterday, I didn't have a class scheduled with her, but today, there would be no avoiding it. She would be my first teacher of the day. After Mom informed me last night of an email she sent to Mrs. Barker and the principal regarding her behavior toward me, I worried all night about what the backlash would be.

At breakfast, I moved my scrambled eggs around on my plate. My stomach was battling the first few bites I had eaten, and nausea was on the front lines of its revolt.

Mom sat at the table checking her work emails. The sound of her fingers clicking away at the keyboard accelerated the throbbing in my head. She wore a gray blue silk blouse that plunged into a deep v, stopping above her breasts. She paired it with a black pencil skirt. Her hair hung loose and glistening, the long layers framing her heart-shaped face.

Sensing my eyes on her, she peering over her laptop. "Are you okay?"

"I'm fine." I gave her a tender smile before going to empty my plate in the compost bin, her eyes following me.

Glancing at the clock, she closed her laptop. "All right, I need to get to work. Now to wake your sister and take her to daycare is going to be the fun part." She drained the last drop of coffee from her mug. "Wish me luck." Rising from her chair, she put her cup in the dishwasher and started to leave the kitchen.

When she got to the doorway, I called to her. "Mom?"

"Yes?" She turned back, eyeing me across the island.

"I can't go to school today." My eyes pleaded for her understanding.

She stared back at me, considering my request, and then her mouth formed into a tight line. "Fine, you can stay home today," she said softly, and then she was gone.

Thirty minutes later, Mom waltzed out of the house with a wailing Ellie tucked under her arm. Ellie aimed to tear down the house in her protest at not wanting to go to daycare.

"Ellie, enough already." Mom said, with a grumble.

"Why does Jules get to stay home? I'm sick too," Ellie said as they went through the garage door.

After they left, I went up to my bedroom. Drawing the curtains closed to shut out the glaring sunlight, I turned on the TV and hit DVR on the remote. Climbing into bed, I searched through the list of previously recorded episodes of *Grey's Anatomy*. Finding the episode I left off on, I hit play. This episode was when the numbskull producers killed off McDreamy.

Barely ten minutes in, the screen began to fade as my eyelids grew heavy and sleep overcame me. When I awoke, the alarm clock read it was past noon.

What the hell? I sat up, staring at the jarring red numbers on the alarm clock. I glanced at my cell phone to find a few missed text from Kaiden.

*Hey, you okay?*

*Jewel?*

*Text me please and let me know all is okay.*

I quickly texted him a reply,

*Sorry, just waking up. I woke with a stress headache and decided to take the day off. I'll see you tomorrow.*

Being the end of lunch hour, he responded instantly.

He texted: *Okay, take it easy. I'll text you after school.*

I looked at his name and placed in my contact list *Kai* with a world emoji and a green heart following his name.

I loved how he made me feel like I was the most important person in his world.

## Kaiden

The school day without her proved to be colorless and lacking. Jewel's text stated she would be absent for the remainder of the day, proving the day would continue at the same lethargic pace. The halls appeared lifeless and empty as I walked from class to class without the echo of her footfalls beside me. Without her bubbly laughter, school lost all appeal, and the monotonous chatter of the students fell like a murmur.

I sauntered into my journalism class after lunch. A class I would never have chosen, but due to my late registration to the school, my options were limited. I slid into my usual desk at the back of the classroom as students filed in behind me. The bore of class was to begin as Mrs. Barker walked into the room and closed the door with a sharp slam behind her.

Today, she chose lime green cat-eyed glasses as a fashion accessory. She was the eccentric type, but I hadn't been caught on her bad side. Leaning back in my chair, I stretched my legs out under my desk as I reviewed her. She was muttering instructions to us, but they fell short on my ears. Her glance met mine, and she held my gaze a moment before turning to her desk.

I checked back in as I saw students flipping through their textbooks and putting their pens to paper. I nudged the girl in front of me to get a quick break down on what I had zoned out on. She shot a look at Mrs. Barker before whispering the instructions. I nodded my appreciation and turned to the page in my paperback textbook.

I racked my brain, trying to come up with an answer to a question in the textbook, when a girl named Chloe rose to go to Mrs. Barker's desk. I didn't know too much about her except she seemed to be the smart, confident type. Mrs. Barker appeared to be fond of her, often signaling her out to read her work to the class. Mrs. Barker would stand back and smile her approval as her golden pupil's voice filled the room.

Now, Chloe approached her desk. Mrs. Barker looked up, and her sulky face noticeably perked up.

"Chloe, what can I help you with?" she said in a hushed voice.

"I heard from Lexi about the email you received from that girl's mother."

"Oh." Mrs. Barker shifted her eyes to me.

I dropped my eyes, and she responded in an even lower voice. My ears strained to eavesdrop on their conversation.

"I know this isn't professional to discuss with a student, but I'm so angry about the email. That student gets under my skin and ticks me off. Can you believe the nerve of her mother? Listen to this." She opened her laptop and read a few lines to her. As she read it, she grew more agitated, and their voices lowered yet again.

They were discussing Mrs. Hart's email! Jewel had told me her mom sent an email. Mrs. Barker was out of line. There was no doubt the conversation which transpired between a student and a teacher was against all protocol.

*Unbelievable!* I shook my head in disbelief at the teacher who abused her authority. There was no way she should get away with this.

## Natalia

The next morning, Natalia Hart was at the school when the doors opened. The Harts were outraged at the audacity of Mrs. Barker's display of unprofessionalism. Mrs. Hart called the school to let them know she was coming. She inhaled and exhaled a deep breath before stalking through the office doors.

The secretary glanced up.

"Good morning," she said with a smile that fell flat.

"Hello, I'm Natalia Hart, and I am here to speak with Mr. Pepper." She flexed her hand by her side.

"Yes, Mrs. Hart. I was the one you spoke to. Usually, we require you make an appointment."

"I understand that, but what I have to say won't wait," she said firmly.

"But—"

"I suggest you don't put me off." Her brows lowered.

"Have a seat, I will call him."

"Thank you." Mrs. Hart took a seat as instructed.

Mr. Pepper came into the main office moments later.

"Mrs. Hart, it's nice to see you." He offered his hand in a limp handshake.

Mrs. Hart nodded and gave a forced smile.

"Do come in," he said and started down the hall to his office.

Once inside, he offered her a seat and rounded his desk and sat down. The heater vent in the ceiling kicked on and ruffled his thinning blond-gray hair, grasping her attention for a brief second.

"What can I help you with?"

She circulated her eyes back to him. "I sent you an email a few days ago about the behavior of Mrs. Barker toward my daughter."

"Yes, we spoke with Mrs. Barker on the matter, and she states it simply isn't true."

"Really?" Mrs. Hart crossed her legs.

"Yes. She says that your daughter is the issue. She disrupts class on a regular basis, and she is defiant."

"Is that so? Well, what we have now is the typical teacher against student issue, isn't it? I know my daughter, Mr. Pepper, and she isn't a liar. I raise my children to be respectful of authority, and if she spoke up in class, there was a reason for it. So do yourself and me a favor and let's not play the he said-she said game. Mrs. Barker is guilty, but we aren't going to be able to prove that, are we?"

"I don't see how we can." He wiggled in his chair at her assertiveness.

"I want you to bring Mrs. Barker down here so we can speak. I emailed you and her as your school requires, but I refuse to go through your insufficient regulations. Honestly, I've never heard of such ridiculousness. When issues arise here between a student and a teacher, we can make an appointment with you but never have I been allowed to speak to the actual teacher. This isn't how schools are run."

"It's the policy we have, Mrs. Hart."

"I'm telling you it's not right, and you need to put a stop to it. Furthermore, a new issue has arisen with Mrs. Barker that you need to be made aware of. She read the email I sent to you and her to some of her students."

"Pardon me?" He arched his brows.

"Yes, you heard me correctly, Mr. Pepper."

"I assure you, you are wrong yet again, Mrs. Hart."

Mrs. Hart slumped back against her chair, and the foot of her crossed leg began to swing viciously. "Unreal!" She looked at him in exasperation. "Mr. Pepper, I grow tired of your excuses for Mrs. Barker."

"Mrs. Barker is part of the community, and her father was the principal of this school before me," he said as if it gave her an excuse to get away with her behavior.

"So this comes down to politics. Is what you are saying?"

"No, I'm telling you that Mrs. Barker is an asset to our school in many ways."

Mrs. Hart scoffed, and her eyes zapped. "I see we will get

nowhere on this issue either." She peered across the desk at him. "Too often, bad teachers slip into the school system. It's teachers like Mrs. Barker who shed a bad light on the teachers whose goals are to truly help guide our children into a productive future. When did school stop being a safe place for our children to grow and learn? It's because of people like you and Mrs. Barker. You appear to be too caught up in the politics and lack the backbone to protect our children from the bullies in this school, including some of your staff. Because I assure you, Mrs. Barker isn't the only one. We've been here multiple times with no results. How can you come here every day and not choose to inspire change? I'll tell you why. It's because you've become complacent. You have not seen the last of me. I will be taking this up with the school board and the media if need be." She stood and with a brief goodbye, she exited the office.

# CHAPTER EIGHTEEN

*Jewel*

A double date night with Kaiden, Finn, and Amy was bound to pull me from my gloom. I'd wasted a day hiding away in defeat. I would not let Mrs. Barker's shortcomings hinder me a second longer.

In my spa-inspired en suite bathroom, Amy and I applied the finishing touches to our appearance for our much-awaited evening out. Adele's smooth, sultry voice drifted from the speakers in my room. We bounced and popped to the beat of "Rumor Has It," singing out a line or two between applications of makeup.

In sync, we leaned forward to outline our lips. My go-to pinky-nude matte shade appeared dull next to Amy's plump, bright red lips. Our eyes met in the mirror, and her beautiful lips curved into a smile that softened her eyes.

"You and Finn appear to be getting pretty cozy. Care to explain that relationship?" I asked.

"I wouldn't call it a relationship. He is a nice guy, and I'm open to seeing where it goes. Honestly, Finn would never have hit my radar before. Even if he had, Lexi would never have allowed it. But I'm trying my best to make up for my past wrongs," she responded while searching through her makeup bag.

I paused my mascara application midstroke and turned to her as she picked up the hairspray can. The bathroom became a haze of hairspray fumes as she applied it to her freshly flat-ironed hair.

I coughed, waving a hand through the air to break up the toxic smog. "But you're not giving Finn a chance out of guilt, are you?"

She set the hairspray on the granite counter and turned to me. I peeked at her in the mirror, and her lovely features dulled as she winced. "I deserve that, I suppose. It's not like I haven't built myself a reputable reputation."

"Amy. I'm sorry. I—"

"No, don't apologize. Your question is valid. I've earned your doubt. I haven't done right by a lot of people. In my weakness, I've hurt people, and I'm trying to figure out how to live with that," she said, her shoulders stooping.

"Well, I think Finn has a mad crush on you."

"I know, and I'm fond of him too. Never would I have dreamed he would be my type, but I find him intriguing and brilliant. Can you imagine being that smart? Like when you wake up and things simply click and you understand things most people never do," she said with a smirk.

"I love how he gets excited when he starts talking about something as boring as atoms, protons, electrons, and neutrons. I swear, he could go on forever. It's like a drug for him."

We laughed at Finn's expense.

He couldn't help it. When you get it, you get it.

"Speaking of drugs, did you hear about Scott Cane? Rumor has it he got caught in the school parking lot dealing drugs to the grade 9 students?" she said as she turned to view the back of her hair in the mirror.

"Doesn't surprise me. I've seen girls exchanging pills in the bathroom."

"I believe it. I once saw Carrie Fox and Lisa Kurt in a bathroom stall shooting up heroin," she said, arching a shapely eyebrow.

"It's sad and kind of depressing," I said, with a long-drawn-out breath. "Why is it that kids don't seem to care? I dream of a future and life after school. These kids live for the moment to numb whatever they are dealing with emotionally. I mean, I've been there. I could have easily taken that way out too. But once you start down that road, it's hard to come back."

"I understand them more than I care to admit. Sometimes, you only want the pain to stop. When you feel so low and helpless, it eats away at you." She paled and tears shimmered in her eyes.

"I know. I get it. Trust me, I do. When I've been at my lowest and darkness consumed me, those dark thoughts overshadowed every waking thought. There was a time when I wanted to end it all. I thought my family would be better off without me." My eyes pooled. "Lucky for me my parents sensed something was off."

"It's obvious you have a strong connection with your family. My parents are great, and they love me. But my mom doesn't want to deal with any emotional stuff. She likes to shove things in the corner instead of dealing with them. I can't talk about my feelings with her, so I deal with them on my own," she said, drawing her lip between her teeth.

"But Amy, that isn't healthy. You have to have an outlet for your feelings."

She glanced away. "I know."

"We could go to a support group together. Maybe one for teens. What do you think?" I said, my eyes beseeching hers.

"Maybe. I'll think about it," she said, her expression closing up.

"Please do. It would be good for us both," I encouraged.

The sound of Finn's horn echoed, and we glanced at each other. Smiles broadened across our faces, and our dismal conversation evaporated. Scurrying to gather our purses, we headed downstairs to greet our dates.

Snowflakes blinked like giant lashes against our cheeks as we stepped outside. Feathery, delicate flurries danced like musical notes in the glimmering streetlights. The woes of our previous conversation left us when we caught a glimpse of Finn's mom's red chariot awaiting us. Our handsome dates leaned casually against the side of the minivan watching our approach.

Kaiden stepped forward and wrapped his arms around me, his silky voice stroking my ears with bliss as he whispered, "Missed you, Beauty."

"What? It's barely been twenty-four hours."

"When you have a good thing, hours seem like years," he

said with a lopsided grin.

"All right, sickos. Break it up," Amy said with a giggle.

Kaiden's arm slid around my waist as we turned to face them. A smile emerged as I looked at the odd pair. Amy stood next to Finn with an elbow resting on his shoulder. She towered above him on any given day, but tonight, with her knee-high boots, she had six inches on him. Give or take.

"Are we going to get this party started or what?" Kaiden said.

"Let's do this. You ladies will receive first-class service tonight," Finn said with a grin as he slid open the back door. With a sweeping hand gesture, he said, "Ladies, please enter your limo."

Amy and I laughed and climbed into the light gray cloth interior van. Finn's five-year-old twin brothers' car seats had been tossed in the rear seat. Evidence of them loomed as a whiff of grease and stale fast food wafted in our noses. In the dim interior light, I brushed the remnants of French fries and melted chocolate candies from the bucket seat.

"Oh, those were in case you got hungry," Finn said as Amy climbed in behind me.

"Hmm, yeah, no, we'll pass," I said with a chuckle, and he slid the door shut.

Kaiden slipped into the passenger seat and glanced over his shoulder at me. He reached back and gave my knee a light squeeze before returning his hand to rest on his own knee.

Finn hurried around the van and slipped behind the steering wheel. He formed his hands into fists and blew on them while shaking through a shiver.

"Brrr. Speak now if you want to change your restaurant choice. Anyone? Somebody, please ..." he said, peering through his rearview mirror at Amy and me. He waited for a second. "All right, we are off to pay top price for fish they don't even cook."

"The things you do for love, hey Finny old boy," Kaiden said, clapping the back of Finn's shoulder.

Finn's carefree laughter fluttered through the van as he backed out onto the street and we were off.

*Half-price Love Boat Tuesdays* a sign read on the door as we entered the sushi restaurant. The door chimed loudly, announcing our arrival to the the owners of the small family-owned business.

"Good day, welcome," greeted a beautiful Japanese waitress dressed in traditional Japanese attire. She showed us to a red booth suited for our party of four. Amy slid in beside me and the guys sat across from us.

The waitress nodded a familiar glance at me. "Back again?"

"Yes, last time I didn't get my fix," I said, with a sheepish grin.

She smiled in pure delight. "Always a pleasure to have you." She took our drink order, offered a tiny bow, and backed away. I loved the mannerisms of the Japanese culture and the humbleness they displayed. My family's travels around the world gave me a love and an appreciation of the beauty of cultures.

"She is onto you and your addiction." Amy nudged my side with her elbow.

"I think Jewel should own shares in this place with the number of times we have been here since I've known her," Kaiden said with a smirk.

He was right. I would die happy if sushi were part of my daily menu. I was guilty of darkening the doors of this establishment a few too many times. I lucked out to obtain a boyfriend who was a sushi junkie too. Amy shared in our love for the raw delectable yumminess. Finn, not so much, but looking to please, he'd agreed to our restaurant choice tonight. Call me crazy, but my thoughts were he aimed to win the approval of the bewitching green-eyed beauty sitting beside me.

"What can I say ... I like what I like." I exaggerated a wink at Kaiden purely for the entertainment of our friends.

They erupted in laughter.

Finn scanned his menu. "You know this thing happening between you two all comes down to chemistry, right? Dopamine and norepinephrine—"

Kaiden clipped Finn's back with his open palm. "We could say the same about you, Finn."

Red seeped up Finn's neck, expanding to the tips of his ears. Finn had dressed with extra swag tonight. The top few buttons of his black, long-sleeve dress shirt were left open, revealing his smooth, dark complexion beneath. Cognac brown fine Italian boots accented his dark-washed jeans. His glossy full hair was slicked back. A spray too much of cologne finished off his "out to take numbers" appearance.

Amy smiled and attempted to ease his embarrassment. "Finn is extra easy on the eyes tonight if you ask me." But her comment only heightened it.

"I'm getting salmon sashimi. How about you guys?" I asked, hoping to deflect the attention from Finn.

"No raw stuff for me." Finn clumsily reached for the glass of water the waitress had set in front of him. He fumbled but caught it in time.

"I'm having shrimp tempura with spicy mayo," Amy informed us.

The waitress returned and took our order.

"Did you guys receive an invite to Chad's party this weekend? It's out at his parents' lake house. You all want to go?" Kaiden eyes twinkled in amusement.

"Not if my life depended on it," I murmured. My fingers drumming the tabletop at the mention of the crude-mannered bad boy.

"What? It would be the perfect entertainment. Don't you think?" Kaiden said with a laugh.

"Because we are that desperate for a life, right? We've all heard how his parties go down. A night of falling down drunks, cocaine, and orgies. Exactly how I want to spend my Saturday." I pulled at the cuffs of my periwinkle silk sweater.

Chad thought he could get away with everything, and most of the time he did. Because his parents bailed him out of any trouble he got into. He was never held accountable for anything, which only seemed to fuel his arrogance.

Amy proved my views as she enlightened us. "At one of his parties last year, it's been rumored he tried to force himself on an exchange student. She only got out of his grip because Lexi walked in. Lexi would never tell me this for the simple fact her boyfriend finding someone else sexually appealing would be unfathomable to her. I believe Lexi played a part in the poor girl transferring to another school." Her face darkened.

"All right, this is a Lexi free night." I narrowed my eyes.

"You're right. Sorry. No L or C names mentioned from here on out." Amy tucked a tendril of hair behind her ear.

That was that. School topics and kids from school were banned from our conversation, and the rest of the dinner date took on a light and refreshing aura. We finished up our date night with the newest action movie release.

# CHAPTER NINETEEN

*Jewel*

The Christmas season tiptoed upon us, bringing with it the welcoming relief of Christmas break. My family transformed our four-thousand-square-foot home into a picture-perfect winter wonderland.

Tonight, we invited the Carters over to share in an evening of Christmas cheer between our two families. Mom made her way around our beautifully decorated family room, offering mini martini glass shrimp cocktails.

"This looks delightful, dear." Kaiden's grandmother praised.

"Thank you," Mom said with a smile.

The wood-burning fireplace crackled and cast a magical glow throughout the room. Our gold knitted stockings dazzled the mantel. In one corner of the room stood an eight-foot Christmas tree. Blinking white lights reflected off the gold and pearl decorations on the tree.

Dad and Kaiden's grandpa were locked in a dreary political conversation about the current prime minister. Mrs. Carter and her mother sat on the L-shaped microsuede sofa. Miles lay on his stomach in front of the fireplace playing a game of solitaire on his smartphone.

Kaiden and I took up residence on the opposite end of the sofa, and Ellie wiggled herself between us.

"Kai, you know that I go to kindergarten next year? Soon, I will be big like Jules," Ellie told Kaiden.

Kaiden chuckled, looking over her head at me. "Yes, Ellie, I know."

"My teacher says I'm real smart too. I may want to be a vet like Jules. Actually, I will probably be just like her." Ellie glanced from Kaiden to me.

"So what does your big sister think of that?" Kaiden said with amusement.

"Her big sister thinks Ellie can be whatever she sets her heart to."

Ellie beamed while tracing my hand with a finger.

I gazed at her, and my heart seized with love. I had begged my parents one too many times for a sister, but the shock of the news that my parents were expecting after Miles and I were half grown had taken us both by surprise. The day we went to the hospital and I'd held this little bundle of pink in my arms, I was mesmerized. When days seemed unbearable, and school days sent me to bed with migraines, I could count on her unconditional love to pull me through.

Ellie stirred beside me. "Oh, I forgot," her small voice chirped as she scooted off the couch. Turning, she widened her eyes as she informed us, "Don't worry. I'll be right back."

She made haste across the light Berber carpet to Dad.

"Daddy, Daddy?" she said urgently, pulling on his pant leg.

He glanced down at her with a disapproving look. "Ellie, I'm talking. It's rude to interrupt."

She didn't let his words deter her and pushed forward with her demand. "Can we give Kai his present yet? I don't want to keep it a secret anymore."

All eyes in the room swiveled to her. Hearty and irrepressible laughter flowed throughout the room.

"You will have to ask Mrs. Carter if she is ready to give him his gift," Dad said.

Ellie went to Kaiden's mom, and bouncing up and down, she squealed, "Can we? Can we?"

"Hold on one second." Mrs. Carter smiled and went in search of her purse. Swiftly, she returned with an envelope in hand. "Ellie thinks there is a matter which needs to be attended to." Mrs. Carter's eyes crinkled. She handed the envelope to a bursting at the seams four-year-old.

"Now? Can I give it to him now?"

"Unless you wanted to wait until tomorrow." A familiar twinkle of a tease formed in Mrs. Carter's eyes.

"No!" Ellie said with a squeak, spinning on her Cinderella dress-up shoes and raced back to us.

Thrusting the envelope at Kaiden, she clasped her small hands in anticipation and sheer delight. "Open it, Kai. Open it!"

"Okay." He grinned at his mom.

He slid his index finger along the seal on the envelope. Pulling out the paper inside, he looked it over and glanced back at his mom. "For real?" His eyes shifted from her to my parents.

Mom found a seat on Dad's lap. She sat with an arm

looped around the back of Dad's neck. They nodded as gigantic smiles plastered their faces.

Confused, I asked, "What is it?"

"It's an airplane ticket. Looks like I'm headed to New Orleans on your family vacation," Kaiden said.

"What?" I grabbed at the paper in his hand. I scanned over the ticket. It was true. "Kai …" My eyes grew big. It must be a dream. One of my favorite destinations had just gotten better. I rose from the couch and hurried to hug and kiss my parents. "You are the best."

"Finally, Dad and I won't be outnumbered," Miles declared.

The room once again erupted in merry laughter.

Five days later, Kaiden's grandfather's driver dropped us off at the airport. Feverish excitement overtook me from the moment I cracked an eyelid this morning. The rapping of my fingers on my knee reverberated throughout the car. The car ride seemed to be taking an eternity. I shifted in my seat again, earning me a glare from Miles.

"Jewel, we aren't going to get there any faster. You might want to chill it back a few strokes."

I yawned, ignoring him.

As the car slowed, I turned to peer out the window.

"Finally," I muttered as we came to a stop outside the Toronto Pearson International Airport.

The driver opened the door, and the early morning bitter cold of -18 degree Celsius slapped us in the face. My breath froze on release. I danced on the spot while I waited for my luggage.

"Okay, let's go before we are frozen into blocks of ice," I said with my hard case luggage in one hand and Ellie's hand clasped in my other. I raced to the revolving doors, keen on getting out of the agonizing cold.

The rest of my group stayed tight on our heels.

"Oh, thank God." I sighed as we stepped into the welcoming warmth of the airport.

The early morning lines went on forever. Eager and tired-faced travelers pushed their load of suitcases on the trollies to the check-in stations. Sleepy babies and small children not pleased with the early disturbance screamed their protest.

"Jules, carry me," Ellie whined.

"No, Ellie you can walk for now."

"But I don't want to. I'm tired." She stomped her foot.

"Ellie, enough," Mom said sternly.

Ellie wandered over to Mom and buried her face into the side of her leg. Soft, pitiful cries hailed from her as Mom gently rubbed her back.

*Great.* We will be the ones with the kid on the plane who cries the whole flight. I longed to crawl back into bed and pull my covers up over my head. When I woke, we would be in New Orleans. This plane ride would suck. Like my kid sister, I wasn't a morning person either, and her whines only added to my growing irritation.

I peered at Kaiden. He had his earbuds in, and his body was grooving to the rhythm of his music. The guy blew my mind. Did he ever have a bad day? No one woke up that content. What special magic did he lace his morning coffee with? I leaned my head on his forearm and yawned.

"Jewel!" someone screeched.

I recognized that voice, and my head flew up.

There was Amy with her suitcase in hand. She waved enthusiastically as she rushed toward me with Finn close behind.

What the heck? What are they doing here? I glanced around my circle of smiling humans to find their eyes were fixed on me. Frowning, I returned my gaze to Amy and Finn.

Amy hurdled herself at me, crushing me in a hug.

"Amy. Hi. What are you doing here? Where are you and Finn headed?"

She pulled back, laughing. "With you, silly." Her high-pitch squeal rebounding throughout the airport.

"With us?"

"Yes, your parents arranged it all."

I jerked my head back to my parents. "Mom?"

"It's time you start living the life you deserve. Dad and I thought what better way to make memories with friends than a trip with the Hart Gang." Her eyes glistened. She wrapped an arm around Dad's waist, beaming up at him.

"Yes, Nat, you pulled it off brilliantly."

"Wow, unreal. I can't believe it. Kaiden and now you guys. New Orleans isn't going to know what hit it." I giggled.

"You know it," Amy sang and squashed me into another hug.

Over her shoulder, I mouthed to my parents, "I love you."

The assurance of my family's love continued to be a guarantee. Friends? I had finally acquired those. The world didn't seem so desolate. Those days were paling in comparison to the whole new world that was becoming mine. So if this was what living life felt like, sign me up.

*Kaiden*

On our arrival in New Orleans, Mr. Hart took charge in herding our caravan of eight through the airport. We effortlessly checked into our hotel in the French Quarter. We had barely unloaded our luggage to our rooms before he had us meeting in the lobby of the hotel.

He grinned like a kid on Christmas morning. "All right, who's up for some charbroiled oysters?"

My stomach bucked at the thought of eating one of the slimy veiny looking critters. I forced back the gag that warned me of its desire to sell me out. I was determined to make an impression on Jewel's family.

A woot erupted from Amy and the Harts. Finn and I peered at each other, the squeamish look in his eyes reflecting my thoughts exactly.

*Ugh.* Sushi, I could handle, but oysters were a whole different thing.

Sometime later, a hostess was showing us to a table on the patio. The therapeutic sound of a live jazz number permeated the evening. I took a look around to find out where it was coming from. Through the black wrought iron fence that encased the patio, I spotted three African American men perched on a bench. One played the saxophone, another the trumpet, and the other a banjo. They played brilliantly and managed to captivate an audience of passersby.

The sun was setting behind the clouds, taking with it the warmth it provided. An invigorating breeze sent a chill seeping through Amy and Jewel. Clad in shorts, flip-flops, and t-shirts, it hadn't been their brightest moment. Beside me,

I could hear the chattering of Jewel's teeth as she curled her body forward, rubbing her goose bump-covered legs.

As Canadians seeking some warmth in the brunt of an arctic freeze, they hadn't dressed for low temperatures. A few of us made the smarter choices of these snow geese, and I removed my light hoodie, tucking it in around Jewel's legs.

Her eyes sparkled and her face illuminated with a sexy smile as she looped her arm through mine, leaning in to steal my body heat.

"Aww," Mrs. Hart said as she laid dreamy eyes on Mr. Hart.

Heat inflamed my cheeks as all eyes turned to me.

A playful gleam ingrained in her dad's blue eyes.

"Young love is a beautiful thing," he chirped, raising his beer to me before growing serious. "Here's to helping my girl see the beauty that lies within her. I thank you."

I lifted my ice water with a nod in her parents' direction,

"Thank you, sir. I'm only lucky she didn't turn me down." I smiled admirably at him.

"Hello, I'm sitting right here," Jewel reminded us with a jab to my ribs.

I doubled over in exaggerated distress.

"Where is my sweater?" Amy narrowed her eyes as she eyeballed Finn.

"Hold on a second, let me pull it out of my butt," he said while holding up his bare arms.

We thundered with laughter.

"If you girls decided to come out half naked, that's on you," Miles added his two cents' worth, earning him a dirty scowl from Jewel.

The waitress arrived with silver trays lined with rock salt

and topped with sizzling charbroiled oysters.

Ellie didn't wait to dig in. She picked up a blistering hot garlicky-lemon oyster from the tray.

"Ow, ow, ow," she squealed as she set it on her own plate. Lifting her fingers to her mouth, she blew on them.

"Couldn't wait for a second, huh?" Mrs. Hart lightly scolded.

Ellie nodded her head in agreement.

Mrs. Hart chuckled. "If you aren't your father's daughter."

Mr. Hart smiled endearingly at his youngest daughter, who peered up at him through adoring eyes.

An ache stabbed at my heart as I watched Jewel's family. I couldn't help but long for what I'd once had.

## Jewel

Mom and Dad retired to the hotel, taking with them a miserably overtired Ellie and leaving us kids to roam the famous Bourbon Street. Neon light signage from restaurants to shops blinked their presence up and down the streets. Racks of t-shirts, along with shelves of souvenirs, lined the sidewalk outside the stores

As far as you could see, tourists packed the narrow streets and sidewalks. People from all walks of life passed by us, earning an occasional head turn from our group.

"Oh, let's stop here," Amy said, spotting something inside a voodoo-inspired shop.

I followed behind her, tucking in my arms as I strolled through the narrow aisles of trinkets. Locating what had grabbed her attention, Amy swung around to face me. A mauve and gold glittered madrigals mask covered her face. Bright purple, green, and yellow feathers along with one peacock feather accented the top of the mask.

Jutting out her chin, she asked, "What do you think?"

"It's bold." I snickered.

"I think I'll get it—"

Commotion from across the store drew our attention to Kaiden, Finn, and Miles. They were laughing and carrying on, creating a ruckus that ricocheted throughout the store.

"Let's go see what they are up to," Amy suggested with a nod of her head.

Joining the guys, we soon found the culprits that'd driven them to hysterics.

Finn wore a pair of gigantic flashy pink sunglasses. Kaiden crowned himself with a Mardi Gras-inspired tiara that read "princess." A yellow boa was wrapped around his neck. Finn and Kaiden stood admiring themselves in the floor-length mirror that hung on the store's storage room door. Miles stood back with an arm propped on a nearby t-shirt rack. His dark eyes laughing, he observed the goons.

"What do you think, Jewel?" Kaiden smirked, blinking repetitively. Spinning for my inspection, he paused to kick up a sneakered heel.

I buried my face in my hands.

Oh, my God. He had no shame.

Looking up, I placed a hand on my hip, grinning at him. "Wow."

"What? Is it too much?" he asked, placing a hand to his O-shaped mouth without a crack of a smile.

His audience exulted with tears of laughter; even Miles couldn't withhold from his charm.

He was the best thing ever. I loved how he made me and the people around me laugh. Life was so much better with my clown of a boyfriend in it. He brought out the best in me.

The guys replaced their props to their rightful places. Wandering the store, we secured some souvenirs before heading back into the congested street.

On our last night in New Orleans, we signed up for a Vampire tour. Dad, never being one to miss a good scare, joined us while Mom opted out with Ellie.

As we stepped in line with the other participants, the towering male tour guide stepped up, and with a long narrow finger, he tossed his oil-slicked black hair over his shoulder.

"Welcome everyone. I will be your tour guide for this one and a half hour tour. Are you wondering what lurks in the shadows? Have you made acquaintances with the undead? Well, tonight be prepared for a night of eerie unsettlement. As we walk, I will share some of the history and legends of New Orleans vampires. We will make a stop at a Vampire tavern and enter the haunted French Quarters. But I warn you, the spider crawl sensation you feel running up and down your back may be more than your own fear." He shivered, and his gravelly booming voice echoed, "All right folks, who is ready to meet some vampires?"

A cheer went up from the participants of the tour. Kaiden cupped his hands around his mouth and let out an ear-splitting howl. People grinned at his response.

This wasn't my idea. If I had my way, we'd be curled up

on a bed at the hotel watching a movie. Chewing on my own heart all night as we wandered the supposedly haunted streets of the French Quarter held no appeal to me.

"All right, let's get this tour started." The tour guide waggled his eyebrows, his beady eyes circling over us as he twisted on his heels. He gave an intentional whip of his ankle-length black trench coat, and we were off.

A cold chill swept up and down my back, and we hadn't even started. The tour guides words rang in my head. No, it wasn't real! My fingernails dug into Kaiden's elbow as we started to move.

"Easy on your grip," Kaiden said with a chuckle.

Through bared teeth, I murmured back, "Your idea. You'll have to deal with the consequences."

He smirked, his eyes glinting. Removing my hand from his arm, he laced his fingers through mine. The firm pressure of his hand in mine sedated the edgy feeling vexing me.

"Scared yet?" Amy said, bumping shoulders with me.

I glanced at her with leery eyes. "What do you think?"

She giggled, keeping her eyes directed ahead. Her smile slipped, and her complexion paled.

"What?" I darted my eyes around.

"Did you see that?" She lowered her voice to above a whisper. Glancing around skittishly, she slowed her steps.

A bowling ball dropped in my stomach, and I swallowed hard. She was playing me, and I wasn't going to let her know she was getting me.

"Good try, Amy. But it's not going to work."

"No, I'm dead serious. I saw something. It was a woman dressed in a flowing dark robe."

I glanced around, the pelting of my heart bruising the

walls of my chest.

A low gnarling chuckle rippled throughout the dark. The trickling of fingers, trailing up my back jarred me.

I screamed and jumped, banging into someone in front of me. My scream vibrated an unrest throughout the group. I swiveled at the sound of laughter coming from behind me as Miles dropped his hand.

Miles and Finn held their stomachs in a fit of laughter. The glow of buoyancy in my dad's eyes pegged him guilt to my party's prank.

"Miles." I grilled. "You're so dumb." Tears filled my eyes.

I wanted to curse them all out, but as the other tour participants joined in the laughter, I stopped my whining. Shooting Miles and Finn a glare, I turned back to the tour guide.

"Sorry about that. These clowns thought I was part of the tour," I said, through a clenched jaw.

The tour guide smiled a knowing smile, unaffected by the disturbance. The rest of the night played out with my family and friends using me as a prop for their amusement.

# CHAPTER TWENTY

*Jewel*

Christmas break was over, and the return to school was inevitable. I glided through the halls on my first day back. Refreshed and ready to face a new semester, I hoped it would follow the trend of positivity of the last.

There was a weightlessness in me as I walked toward my locker. New Orleans had been everything I wanted and more. The memories would stay with me for a lifetime. I aimed to live in the moment, and not focus on the high school social experience I'd missed. In the quiet times, it plucked at me and found empty space in my head. What if this was my life all along? What if the void of friends and years of loneliness were only a dream. Who would I be today?

I caught sight of Jess leaning against the lockers, chatting with Lexi and Chad. Chad's hand callously cupped Lexi's butt. No discretion. No worry of being caught. His narcissistic ways never ceased to amaze me. He was a loser to the hundredth degree, and I loathed the ground the three walked on.

Jess's cunning blue eyes met mine. Her lips twisted into a sour expression as she leaned over to say something to Lexi. Lexi and Chad rotated to scrutinize me. Dropping my eyes, I felt my muscles tense as I passed by.

They attacked!

Her foot came out, and I tried to catch myself, but it was to no avail. My books sailed through the air and the jolting impact of the floor knocked the wind from me. Bleach from the recently mopped floors burned my nostrils. I stiffened as their laughter slashed through my ringing ears.

"Hart, did you forget to tie your shoelaces?" Lexi jeered.

Passing students scanned over me as they continued down the hall. No one offered me a hand up or reached to gather my books. A flush crept over my cheeks, and my chin dipped. Searing tears glided down my cheeks.

You were a fool, Jewel. A damn fool.

I should have known better than to anticipate school would be anything different. Why did I let my walls down? The ones I spent years fortifying? Lexi and her friends didn't need to apply their hatred on me. I'd become good at doing that myself. I always had been.

Rising to my knees, I scooted along the hallway to gather my belongings.

"The view keeps getting better and better." Chad's crude comment scored another mark on the destruction board labeled *Jewel's Life*.

Where was my phone?

I scurried around, searching under the dust filled cracks at the bottom of the lockers. The bell rang, causing a charge of students to hurry to their first class. They blew past me without a second thought of aiding the girl scrambling along on the floor. Tears of frustration engulfed me, and I began to sob. It was pointless.

"Looking for this?" Lexi tapped her black high-heeled boot on the floor beside my phone. Jess pored over me, grinning like the spawn of Satan. Chad leaned back against a locker, folding his arms across his chest as he watched the scene unfold before him.

My pulse quickened as I feverishly brushed at my tears. I'd given them exactly what they'd wanted. By showing them my vulnerability, they basked in my demise. The last thing I ever wanted was to show *her* what she'd reduced me to.

I stood, dusted myself off, and edged toward her to retrieve my phone. Jess and Lexi began to play a game of cat and mouse. Kicking my phone back and forth until I pulled back and refused to play.

"All right, fine, you win. Such a baby. Here you go." Lexi rolled her eyes and nudged the phone toward me. But as I bent over to get it, she ground the heel of her boot into the screen.

*Crunch.* I gawked at the shattered screen under her heel.

My limbs grew heavy like iron shackles were snapped closed around them. A quiver captured my chin. As if in slow motion, I lifted my eyes to meet Lexi's.

"You going to cry again?" Jess taunted.

I tuned her out and kept my eyes pinned on Lexi.

"Why, Lexi? We used to be friends." My voiced clogged with emotion.

Lexi bared her teeth, and her face contorted with years of a pinned-up grudge.

"You know why."

"Because of that? I tried to save you from yourself." I screamed.

"You should have minded your own business." Her venom seeped from her.

"I cared about you," I cried. "You were my friend. I saw then, just as I see now, that you are broken. I couldn't stand by and watch you reduce yourself to those smutty naked pictures you were sending around to the guys at school. I understood you were dealing with the emotions of your dad leaving. You tried to get attention whatever way you could. It's not like I even told anyone else. I only told you to stop. And reminded you, you were better than that. Then out of nowhere, you turned on me. The one who cared enough to say something." The urgency to be heard by her was overpowering.

She laughed at me, and an ugliness covered her pretty face. "Be gone, you worthless twit." With a dismissive wave, she brushed off my feelings like a pestering house fly.

The assault of tears again terrorized the corner of my eyes. I would not be a victim to their bloodbath of my sanity. Aimlessly, I turned and ran toward the exit. I heard someone call my name, but I kept running down the corridor and out the front doors of the school.

I didn't stop until I reached the bleachers at the baseball field. Sitting down, I buried my face into my bare arms. My body began to sway back and forth, ignoring the burn of the frozen bleacher beneath me.

My soul lurched and dispersed into a vacant puff. A scream of agony burst from my lips. Why me? Why? What had I done to deserve this? How could Lexi still be angry about something that happened years ago? I'd only tried to help her. I'd done nothing wrong.

The crunching of the snow under someone's footfalls ceased my cries. While holding my breath, I waited to see who had intruded on my misery. The footsteps made their way up the bleachers, and the intruder sat down beside me.

"Jewel?" His voice was thick with emotion. The tenderness of his hand on my arm warmed the impending frostbite.

My head snapped up. "Kaiden?" I choked as he opened his arms, and I obliged the zeal of his embrace.

He encompassed me in the protection of his arms. The muscles in his body were tense, and I perceived the hard set of his chin as he rested it on my head. His freshly washed hoodie soaked up my tears. I lay in his arms until my sobs lessened, turning into hiccups.

Moving me out of his embrace, he searched my face with his dark eyes. Using his fingers, he brushed back my tear-drenched hair that was pasted to my face.

"What happened? I've never seen you like this. Finn said you blew past him, and you appeared to be extremely upset."

I waved a hand wildly in the air. "It's what always happens. I can never catch a break. I'm so mad at myself. I'd hoped … I thought this year had finally been my turn around. I had you. I had Finn and Amy. Foolishly, I thought it would stop. I don't get it, Kai. What is it about me that makes me a target? What? What?" My voice elevated. "I want to fade away. Fade from their sight. The pain I feel, I no longer want to feel it anymore. I can't … I can't feel it anymore."

His eyes shifted at my words, and he clasped my elbows tightly with his hands.

"Stop it! Don't talk like that." He swallowed hard.

"You don't know what it's like, Kaiden. This has been thirteen years. Not one or two but thirteen years of a living hell. It never stops. I need it to stop." Hysterics ravaged my body.

"Jewel, what happened?"

Devoid of all emotion, I related the event to him.

His mouth unhinged then closed abruptly. The clank of his teeth echoing.

I hugged my arms to my body. The cold of my exposed arms set in, and the frozen metal of the bleacher beneath me jarred me.

Kaiden removed his coat and wrapped it around my shoulders. I eagerly placed my arms in the sleeves. Thankfully, he still wore his hoodie, providing him with some barrier to the cold.

My head pounded from the stress and the tears I had spent. I squeezed my eyes tightly shut. The brightness of the sun on the blanket of snow glared like a nail to my temple.

"I need to go home."

"Right after we deal with this," he said through bared teeth.

I jerked my eyes to look at him. "What?"

"Let's go." He jolted up, leaping down the bleachers, pausing at the bottom to look back at me.

I remained still.

"Let's go. Now!"

I moved. Not because he demanded it but because the chill in his eyes frightened me.

He pivoted on his heels and headed toward the school.

"Kaiden. Wait, stop."

He didn't listen. His stride length was twice the length of mine. I ran in hopes of reaching him, but he charged through the front doors. The door swung shut behind him.

# CHAPTER TWENTY-ONE

*Kaiden*

S he called to me. But I kept going, rage inhabited my mind and compressed my body. I would not let Lexi and her crew get away with it. This school needed to deal with the brutal truth of what Jewel had suffered. What they continued to neglect to properly deal with. I flung the office door open.

The two secretaries behind the desk swung around, their eyes wide and bulging.

The nearest secretary's voice hitched as she asked, "Excuse me, can I help you?"

"I want to talk to the principal this minute!" I demanded, running my fingers through my hair. I knew I looked like a raving lunatic, but I didn't care.

This had to stop.

The air flow to my brain became restricted by Jewel's words. Immense pressure snatched at my throat.

She would not become a statistic. I would not allow it.

"I suggest you calm down." The secretary straightened her lips into narrow taut lines.

The breeze of the door swinging open alerted me to Jewel's entrance. I set my eyes on the secretary in front of me. The grasp of urgency in Jewel's fingers on my arm did not sway me from the single-minded mission I was on.

My jaw twitched. I remained silent for half a second.

"What is your name?" inquired the dark-haired secretary, peering over her thin wired lenses.

"Kaiden. Kaiden Carter."

Why would they know my name? In a school of hundreds of students, we were simply a head count.

"What is the matter, Mr. Carter?"

I heaved a sigh. "Like I stated, I want to see the principal."

"I'll check if he is available—"

"He needs to make himself available." I asserted, firmly.

Her expression pinched. "Like I said, I will check his schedule."

I seethed, "No, I'm telling you, you have a matter that needs someone to give a fuck about."

The secretary immediately picked up the phone and made a whispered called.

"Kaiden." Jewel's voice cracked.

I half turned to her. I was vibrating on my toes as adrenaline seeped through my veins.

"No, Jewel. They need to listen."

This school would wake up and pay attention. I wasn't leaving this office until they did. They could carry me out in a straight-jacket, but I would have my say.

From the hallway that led to other offices, the principal

entered, "Mr. Carter? Jewel? What is the problem?" His eyes glanced from me to her.

Clearing my throat and squaring my shoulders, I said, "We have to speak to you about an incident which took place with Lexi, Chad, and Jess."

Jewel stiffened beside me, and I took her hand in mine. Her palm was sweaty, and she trembled, but she stood silent.

The principal grew impatient. "Let's move this along. I have a meeting in a few minutes."

I stared at him across the mahogany stained u-shaped desk. His emotionless slate-gray eyes returned my stare. His chair creaked beneath him as he leaned forward and folded his hands on the desk.

"You'd better have a good reason for charging into the office and scaring the staff, Mr. Carter," he commanded.

I continued my stare as I studied the school official before me. His receding hairline drew attention to the popping veins in his forehead.

I bit back the words I wanted to say. "We'll get straight to the point. Jewel, why don't you inform Mr. Pepper what took place in the hallway," I said, never taking my eyes off him.

Jewel repeated what had taken place, and Mr. Pepper's faced revealed his visible shock.

"All right, I will see to this."

"But how, Mr. Pepper? How will you make it different than all the other times my folks have been in here? A day or two suspension to a student is a reward, not a punishment.

Your methods have to change," Jewel said.

"You're a student, Jewel. Let me handle how this school is run," he said arrogantly.

"I mean no disrespect, but as a student, I should have a voice," she replied. But I heard the falter in her voice, and this only fueled the bubbling rage inside me.

"Mr. Pepper, I'd like to know how many suicides this school has had in the past five years?"

"What?" His chin dropped, and his Adam's apple rapidly moved up and down.

"I asked. How many suicides has this school had in the past five years?"

A hardness crept into his eyes. "I'm not deaf, young man. I heard what you asked. What is your point?"

I heaved a heavy sigh. "Teen suicide is ravaging the world. You can't turn on a TV, turn a page in a paper, or search the internet without seeing some poor kid who has been tormented by peers until they feel they have no choice but to end their lives."

"Yes, it's a terrible thing." He sat with a poker face while the cords in his neck revealed his annoyance of me. But he compelled his body to stay rigid and detached.

"Yet you continue to act like it doesn't exist. You are aware of it in your school. The school, the school board, entrusted into your care. The students walking these halls everyday inflict pain and cruelty daily on students they view as less than them. Sure, you can't be everywhere at once, but it doesn't give you the right to become indifferent. Right here, students are traumatized by the effects of bullying, and you and your staff allow it to continue. Heck, it happens with some of the staff who run this school."

"Pardon me?" he scoffed. "I warn you, Mr. Carter, you'd better choose your words wisely. Are you accusing the staff of bullying the students?"

"Yes, some do. I've witnessed your staff and staff at the other schools verbally degrade students when they are stressed or simply in a mood. Teachers are human just as much as the next person. In this world, ill-mannered people roam in all forms."

"Name the staff personnel you hold this claim against." His face reddened.

"Mrs. Barker, for one. I've seen her demean students and on more than one occasion."

"I'm sure you misunderstood—"

"Mr. Pepper, I know what I heard." My pulse raced.

His nostrils flared, his lips tightened into a straight line, and he remained silent. His silence allowed me to deliver my final thought.

"In your school, students are dying inside from the treatment by peers and by the teachers who shouldn't see the inside of another classroom. How can you turn a blind eye? How many more kids' blood will be on your hands and the hands of your staff? I won't sit by and witness kids I care about walk that scary road alone. I refuse to be silent." Grief overshadowed me. I stood and pushed back my chair to leave.

Jewel stood and took my hand in hers.

At the door, I turned to him.

"The number is three," I said.

"Huh?" he asked.

"Three students in the past five years. Three too much. Don't you agree?" I asked grimly before opening the door and walking out.

# Jewel

My enlarging heart thrashed against my breastbone. Tunnel vision set in as we walked out of the office. Blocking out the activity going on around me and the sizzling eyes of the secretaries as we walked by.

In the hall, his stern gaze probed mine. He placed his hands on his hips and paced in circles, mumbling under his breath.

Using my teeth, I picked off the last of the pearl-pink nail polish from my fingernails.

"Thanks, Kai. Thank you for standing up for me. You have no idea how much your strength and support means to me," I said gently.

"Yeah, you're welcome," he said dryly, coming to stand in front of me. Cupping my shoulders with his hands, he planted a kiss on my forehead. "If you don't stand up for yourself, you will continue to be the gum on the bottom of people's shoes."

"I know, but when the school continues to do nothing about it, it only makes it a waste of energy," I grumbled.

"I've seen enough of this place for the day. Get your things. You can call your mom from my phone," he said solemnly. His beautiful eyes usually swept me away with the light and hope within them. I swallowed at the dull emptiness harrowing them.

My heart quickened.

"Okay," I replied meekly. Sorrow wedged deep in my stomach.

I gathered my things and followed him to his car. Phoning Mom, I let her know I'd be going home. I heeded the panic in her voice when she asked me why. My voice cracked, and sobs overtook me. She asked no more questions and said she was on her way.

Hanging up, I glanced at Kaiden. His eyes were focused straight ahead.

I slid down in my seat and stared out the window. A haze choked out the flow of my thoughts. The blinking of my eyelids seemed foreign as if the movement belonged to someone else.

No words passed between us. The radio broadcaster's voice pierced through the car. We pulled into my drive. I sat for a moment longer, then unbuckled my seat belt and climbed out. A push of the door with my foot closed it with a thud behind me.

I strolled toward the house, but the sound of his door opening caused me to freeze midstep.

"Jewel." The concern in his voice pulled at me.

I swiveled to face him. His face was unreadable.

"Yes?"

Circling the car, he hurried to me, furiously crushing me to his chest.

"I can't lose you. Please, know I love you."

He loved me? My tummy flipped. He loved me. I clung to him, my nails clutched at his shirt.

His jacket? Oh, my God.

Pulling back, I removed his jacket.

"I forgot I was wearing it. Here, put this on."

"Jewel," he shrieked in exasperation.

My eyes snapped up to his. "What now?"

"Today. Is what. You scared me."

"What? How?" I remained dumbfounded by his behavior

since the bleachers. I knew he was mad about Lexi and her gang, but why did it seem it reflected back on me?

"You said you wanted to fade, and you wanted it to stop—"

Uhh? What was he saying? Oh ... he thought.

"No, Kaiden. I was hurting. I wouldn't do that. I won't do that. I promise you. I may be broken today, but I won't let this take my life. I've been there, and I'm not going back. I refuse to go back," I confirmed.

"Oh, thank God." Fiercely and unyielding, he once again captured me into his arms.

He no longer comforted me, but I him.

"Don't ever leave me. Don't let life get that bad. You are stronger than that," he whispered into my hair. His hot, passionate breath sent tingles throughout my body.

"I promise you."

At that moment, I realized he needed me in his life as much as I needed him.

Mom's car raced into the driveway and screeched to a stop. She'd barely put the car in park before she sprinted across the icy drive in her heels.

"Jewel, honey, what's wrong." Her gaze flitted from me to Kaiden.

"I'm okay, Mom." I stepped back.

She reached out and pulled me into her shielding embrace.

"Someone needs to tell me what happened, and you'd better make it fast." Her eyes sizzled with determination.

"I'll tell you everything," I said.

"She'll be good with you, Mrs. Hart?" Kaiden asked.

"Yes, Kaiden. I'll be here."

"All right. I'm going to go home." His eyes finding me, he said, "Call me."

"Okay."

Mom and I stood watching him until his car disappeared down the street before she spoke.

"What happened, Jewel?"

I quickly filled her in on everything. A grimace controlled her mouth, and she pulled her jacket tighter as she listened.

"I'm sorry this happened, Jewel. As I've told you time and time again, it's not you, it's them. They're angry inside, and by picking on you, it somehow makes them feel better. It isn't right, and I don't fully understand it either. But lack of parenting in these kids' lives has a part to do with it. I do want to say I'm extremely proud of you and Kaiden for standing up against bullying and for reporting those kids. It took guts for you two to stand up to Mr. Pepper." She wrapped her arm around my shoulder as we turned toward the house. "I will be in touch with the school to make sure Mr. Pepper deals with it."

"For some reason, I believe you will do just that." I grinned, pulling her closer.

# CHAPTER TWENTY-TWO

*Lexi*

The little snitch ratted on them to Mr. Pepper, and he'd banned them from the upcoming high school Valentine's dance. She didn't honestly care as school events were lame compared to the fun they could have on any given night.

Her loathing of Jewel magnified with her success in taking Amy to her side. The likeness of Jewel and Amy sickened her.

Weak and useless.

In a short amount of time Amy had hung out with Jewel, she reeked of happiness, and it drove Lexi crazy. Now not only did Jewel have the perfect home life, but she also had the hottest guy in school and a great guy at that. She was surrounded by friends who actually cared about her even if it were that nerd Finn and Amy. No matter how much she aimed to make Jewel feel like shit, she still came out on top.

Lexi sat on the couch beside Chad in his guest house. Jess, Eric, and a few of their other friends lounged in chairs around the small living room.

Chad bent down and snorted the cocaine on the table. He leaned back against the couch, closing his eyes he sighed. "Anyone want a hit?" He opened his eyes and made some weird grunting noises before he asked, "Eric?"

"No way, man. I told you, I'm not messing up my life with that stuff." Eric pushed himself up off the couch.

"Where are you going?" Chad laughed.

"I got things to do. I'll see you around."

Chad called him some choice names as he went out the door.

"What about you, Lexi?" He turned to her.

"No."

"Come on, don't be a whiner." He pulled her closer.

"Chad I said no." She pushed out of his snare.

"You're so weak," he said with a snort of disgust.

"I'm not weak," she fumed.

"Then take a hit."

"I said no. So drop it." She jumped up and headed toward the door but stopped within a few paces. "Why don't you ask Jess. She seems willing to do whatever you ask."

"What's that supposed to mean?" Jess wailed.

"Don't play dumb, Jess. I know you're sleeping together." She glared at the girl who was supposed to be her friend.

"I ... I ... Lexi, listen." She stumbled.

"Save your breath, Jess." Lexi stormed from the house.

In her car, she rested her forehead against the steering wheel. The tears that fell darkened her light blue jeans. They deserved each other. Lexi hated them both. But without them, she had no one, and it frightened her.

# Jewel

We pushed on into February. The incident on the first day back to school carried mild repercussions for Lexi. Kaiden's conversation with the principal resulted in the school hanging more 'No Bullying' campaign posters. The school attempted to make an impact on "The Effects of Bullying" with an assembly in the gymnasium. But after the initial effort, it fell short and soon faded away, as if forgotten.

Today, we were going out to celebrate Amy's 18th birthday with a girls' day out. I pulled up in front of her house at a quarter past ten on a Saturday morning.

Amy's two-story, red brick home resembled the rest of the houses on her block. The exquisite handcrafted wooden doors with three-quarter length stained glass panes gave the home its uniqueness. A charcoal gray stamped concrete drive wrapped around the back of the house. Well-groomed hedges and trees surrounded the front of the house, leaving the impression someone in Amy's home had a green thumb.

Turning my car off, I jogged up to the front door and rang the doorbell. Moments later, the door swung open and Amy's mom, an attractive woman maybe in her forties, greeted me with an inviting smile. Her angled bob of champagne-blond hair softened her square jawline.

"Hello, Jewel," she said, opening the door wider and welcoming me in.

"Hello, Mrs. Kent."

"It's nice to see you again. Amy was mentioning the other

day how good a friend you have been to her. She was also filling me in on how talented you are."

"Mom," Amy playfully groaned as she ambled in from a room to the left of the foyer. "Don't tell her of my secret infatuation with her."

Arching a brow, I smirked. "Interesting."

"Stop." Amy giggled.

"All right, birthday girl. Are you ready to put a dent in our bank cards?" I asked.

"Absolutely," Amy chimed in. Planting a quick peck on her mother's cheek, she grabbed her gold-chain strapped emerald green purse.

"You girls have fun," her mom called after us.

We turned and waved at her.

"See you soon," Amy yelled back.

On the drive to the mall, I sat listening to her carefree chatter. Over the past few months, I found great joy in watching her become a girl who was no longer held back by superiority. As her confidence grew, it gave me a sense of hope. Hope that she valued herself for the amazing person she was. If I had to summarize Amy in two words, it would be compassionate and humble. If I were the author of life, I would've written our script as being friends from the start. Together we could've been a united front. Maybe then … broken wouldn't define our makeup.

Lexi had taken Amy's abandonment as a direct attack on her and targeted Amy with a vengeance. From staredowns in the hallway to threatening notes, which kept appearing and were becoming more aggressive over time. If it wasn't at school, it was on social media or through text. It was spiraling out of control, and it concerned me more with each passing day.

"Do you know how great it feels to be yourself?" Amy was saying when I zoned back in.

"It's everything. Because what's life if the people in it don't allow you to be you?" I replied.

"That's the thing I love about you. You are so confident and sure about yourself."

I jerked my head toward her. "Are you crazy?"

Her eyes widened. "What?"

"What I mean is, no, you're wrong. I'm the total opposite of that. Confident is one thing I'm not."

"I disagree, Jewel. You are the meaning of strength. You've wandered solo for so long. When you get knocked down, you brush yourself off and get back up. Life's given us all our own set of challenges, but you somehow press on. I'm not like you." Her expression dropped.

"Amy, school has been a pit of vipers since the day I walked in. This year has been no different. The only difference is, I've finally been blessed with friends. I draw my strength from that. In finding you guys, I feel like I've won the lotto."

Awe transformed her face, and she smiled a genuine smile. "Well, it's nice to be considered a winning ticket."

"That you are, my friend. That you are." I laughed as we pulled into the mall parkade.

We shopped until my feet were raw from the rubbing of my gray suede ankle boots, crushing our shopping budget. We moved on to our last splurge of the day. Pedicures and my gift to Amy.

I rubbed my aching feet over the hot stones. The aesthetician poured a blend of soothing eucalyptus mint oil into the warm sudsy water.

Oh, yes. I sighed, relaxing back into the massage chair. Closing my eyes, I breathed deeply.

Lost in thought, I quietly sat, tracing one of my big toes over the bottom of the basin. Days like today, I was thankful for the people who'd become a big part of my life. I blinked away the tears marking my vision. Happiness was no longer so foreign to me.

A hand on my arm grasped my attention.

"Jewel, what's wrong?" Amy asked.

"Nothing. I'm good." I feigned a catching smile. "I'm feeling grateful to have you. Shopping, lunch, and now a pedicure. What more can a girl want, right?"

What I wanted to say, but didn't, was this was a first for me. Never had I experienced a day like this. A day where I was one of the girls cruising through the stores laughing and trying things on. Saying to her friend, "You should totally get that," or "That's adorable." Then we would have lunch and maybe see a show. No, I didn't tell her any of this because what if … what if she saw me as others often did. I couldn't lose her.

Amy's phone sang out her ringtone for a text.

"Most likely my mom wondering when we are coming home. She is cooking me a birthday supper tonight. You know, Jewel, this truly is the best day I've had in a long time."

She beamed as she dug through her purse for her phone. Locating it, she swiped the screen with a finger to read the text.

The smile plastering her face a second ago slipped. The color drained from her face, and her lower lip began to tremble.

"Amy? What is it?"

She shoved the phone at me.

I read the text: *Happy Birthday, I wonder if your real mom remembers? Probably not.*

A sharp breath caught in my throat as I peered at the message. I read it again, making sure my eyes weren't playing games with me. There was no phone number assigned to the text, but we knew exactly who the message was from.

"Amy—"

"Don't try, Jewel. This is what I deserve." She lamented, turning to watch the aesthetician apply the first coat of mauve nail polish on her toes.

"You will not silence me, Amy. The text is evil. No one deserves to be told that. No one. Girls are vindictive and sometimes plain hateful. We should be lifting each other up, yet we tear each other down. Life would be so much better if everyone would only realize this."

With one text, what had been a wonderful day turned upside-down. Dispirited, Amy withdrew into herself and didn't speak for the remainder of the pedicure. Only when we got in the car, did she turn to me.

Her expression demonstrated the battle taking place in her mind.

"I want to show you something only my mom knows ... okay?"

"Okay."

She lifted her pale blue sweater and revealed the skin beneath. Years of self-cutting tattooed her pale skin.

My heart sank, pins and needles sheathed me.

Her pain lacerating my heart. I repressed a groan.

"I'm sorry, Amy, that life made you think you had no choice. I'm sorry for the adults who failed you and for the fact life isn't fair. Also, for the failures of the parents who raised the kids who target you. I'm sorry for it all. I wish I could take it all away."

She toyed with the diamond pendant that hung around her neck. "This is like second nature to me and has become part of who I am. I think I started cutting around the time my real dad brought his drug dealer to my bedroom. When I was around six years old. My father owed him money or something, and I was the payment. It's sick that your own father could do this to his own child." She glanced at me with hollow, preoccupied eyes.

I reached for one of her trembling hands and clasped it firmly in mine. Rubbing my thumb lightly over the top of hers, I opened my mouth to speak but closed it.

"This became my release from the numbness and emptiness. As twisted as it may seem, it makes me feel something." She began to weep, her body shaking with raw and unrestrained emotion.

My mind screams out for the six-year-old Amy and for the girl who sat in my car shattered and hurting beyond what I could ever imagine.

I didn't know what to do or what to say to help her. No matter how much pain and hurt I'd dealt with in my life, hers was so much worse. My throat burned with the rising bile scratching at the back of my throat.

Amy ... my God.

As we turned into Amy's drive, the sorrowfulness of earlier dissipated. We squealed in delight at the shiny black BMW sitting in front of her house. An oversized red bow adorned the top of the roof.

Amy's eyes bounced from the car to me.

"Is that for you?" I asked.

"I don't know," her voice squeaked as she glanced again at the car.

The front door of her house flew open, and her mom and dad hurried out.

I peered at Amy. "By the look on your folk's faces, I'm going to say that gorgeous car is yours."

"Let's go find out."

My car barely stopped rolling before Amy threw open the door and jumped out.

I exited my car in time to hear her dad ask, "Amy, what do you think?" He tilted his head in the direction of the car.

"It's amazing. Whose is it?" she asked.

He opened his mouth to speak, but her mom beat him to the punch. "It's yours, honey!" she cried, clapping her hands together.

"For real?" Amy's voice cracked as she ran a hand over the hood of the car in awe.

"Yes, call it a birthday present slash graduation present," her dad said with pride.

Amy walked around the car, and her eyes glistened with welling tears. The curve of her mouth tucked up into a lavish smile. She raced back around the car and threw herself into her dad's arms.

She crushed him to her, his glasses twisted lopsided on his face.

Her mom stepped in, draping her arms around them both.

My eyes refused to cooperate, and tears skimmed my cheeks at the beauty of what Amy was experiencing. This was what she deserved. The love of a family. She had been conceived by others, but this was where she belonged. She was handpicked by them. Loved for everything she was and wasn't.

Amy's eyes were bathed in elation when she turned to face me.

"Jewel, it is mine," she gushed.

"Well, I guess we know who is driving to school tomorrow," I piped in, and we shared a laugh.

Before making my departure, I locked Amy in a hug and gingerly murmured for her ears only, "You are loved, Amy. You are worthy of all this." I pulled back. "Don't ever question that, okay?" I gazed into her tear-rimmed eyes.

She bobbed her head up and down. Her lashes fluttered, cutting off her falling tears.

"Thank you, Jewel. You simply are the best friend a girl could ever ask for."

"You'd better believe it, baby." I lifted my nose in the air, securing a giggle from her.

"Well, I'm off. Until next time," I told her parents. "I'll see you tomorrow. When we turn heads driving to school in that." I nudged my head at her new car.

"For sure," Amy said with a smile.

As I drove away, my thoughts returned to Amy's enlightenment of her past. It seemed surreal as if I'd seen it in a movie. I imagined a giant eraser erasing the scene from her life.

If only.

At the end of school the next day, I found Amy waiting at my locker. Her face broke into a wide grin when she spotted me.

"Hey, Jewel. I'm starving. Did you want to grab a bite to eat? I haven't eaten today. I bought these pants a size smaller, and if I eat, they cut off my circulation." She sucked in her perfectly flat stomach while undoing the top button.

I admired her skintight, dark green pants which showed off her decade's long legs. She'd paired them with four-inch microsuede boots.

I chuckled with a shake of my head as I shoved my textbooks in my locker. "I don't understand how you can wear those heels in the winter. I would break my neck for sure."

"But they look cute with this outfit. Don't you think?" she asked, nibbling on her bottom lip.

"Yes, they do. I'm only saying when I see girls wearing heels in the winter, it makes me nervous. I'm just waiting for them to slip. So don't worry, you look stunning as always."

She brightened. "Understood. What do you say about us getting out of here?" she beamed.

Outside, Kaiden and Finn met us. Amy pounced on them about going out.

"We are thinking of grabbing a bite to eat. Do you guys want to come?"

I hadn't agreed to go, but I didn't want to burst her bubble.

"I'm in," Finn said as he took in Amy's appearance.

"Good. What about you Kaiden?" Amy asked.

Kaiden stood flirting with me with his eyes. "I'm in," he agreed.

I spoke up. "Hate to break it to you'll, but if I'm going, I have to bring Ellie."

Finn simpered, "Fine by us."

Amy grinned, twirling her new keys in the air. "I'll drive."

Kaiden slung an arm around my shoulder, and we meandered to the parking lot.

Finn prattled on about a biology experiment his class performed on the dissecting of a pig.

My stomach furled at his in-depth description. I'd have to toughen up my squeamish stomach if I aimed to fulfill my ambitions of becoming a vet.

"Mr. B said we will be dissecting a lamb heart next," Finn informed us with a smirk at the grossed out look painted across Amy's face.

"Mr. B rocks. He has a way of making his lessons seem effortless," I praised. Mr. B taught me biology this semester, and I looked forward to his class. All students were equal to him. He was passionate about teaching and took pride in his students' success.

Our chatter halted when a loud gasp escaping Amy's lips.

"Amy, what is it?" I eyed her with concern.

She raised a hand to her mouth, and tears welled in her eyes. Lifting her other hand, she pointed in front of us, our eyes following her hand.

Students had started to gather around Amy's new car. Spray painted on the driver's door from bumper to bumper in red paint were the words whore and slut.

I gasped. "What? Who …?"

"Assholes," Finn cursed, his face turning a scarlet purple.

Amy's sobs saturated the space around us. She melted into me, and I cloaked her shoulders with an arm.

"This will never stop … never." Tremors overtook her body, and I staggered to hold her dead weight.

Finn and Kaiden charged into the group of laughing and pointing students. Accusations fell like liquid fire as they tried to find out who'd do something so abominable. The students raised their hands, pleading they had nothing to do with it.

As they dispersed, I caught sight of Lexi and Jess. They strolled by, smirking deliberately at us. I couldn't help but think those two were behind this horrendous act of viciousness.

Kaiden jaw locked and his eyes flashed. "Come on, Finn. Let's go see if they got anything on the cameras." He stalked back toward the school.

Shocked at the occurrence, and fighting his own rage, Finn didn't move until Kaiden called out, "Finn, come on."

"Coming," he shouted and took off running.

Amy pushed back. "I need to call my dad and let him know. He will need to inform the insurance company." Amy's eyes looked through me as she pulled out her phone.

We suspected Lexi and Jess had done this, and by the satisfied look they shot our way, my guess was they had. This was the ultimate low. Oh, I'm sure they never physically did the deed themselves. But they probably convinced some poor lovestruck kid to do it for them.

Twenty minutes later, Amy's parents showed up to deal with the vandalism. I was running late for picking up Ellie from daycare, so once I knew Amy was in good hands, I left.

Later that night, I called Amy to check in on her.

Her voice sounded labored and strained. "Hello."

"Hey, Amy, I wanted to check in on you and find out how things went."

"It will be taken care of with insurance. The school checked the security cameras, but as expected, the cameras didn't reach that far. " Her voice was raspy as if she'd been crying.

"How are you doing?" I said, knowing that she wasn't faring well.

"I'm fine. Just tired. I'm beyond sick and tired of it all. Life shouldn't be this hard."

"I know, Amy. Trust me, I do."

"It's too much sometimes." Her voice hitched as her attention seemed to drift.

"We are almost done with school, Amy. Only four more months and we will leave it far behind. It will be over soon."

"Yeah, you're right." Tears broke her voice.

"I will pick you up for school in the morning, okay?"

"Okay," she softly replied. "Jewel?"

"Yes?"

"Thanks. Thanks for being my friend."

"Back at you," I said before we hung up.

# CHAPTER TWENTY-THREE

*Jewel*

The next morning, we woke to a fresh dusting of snow, and it was still coming down. The skies were gray and laden with the promise of a stormy day. For a day like today, I decided on yoga pants and a hoodie. I combed my hair back into a ponytail and headed downstairs.

Miles sat at the island chatting to Dad, who leaned against the counter in front of him.

Mom and Ellie must still be upstairs?

I slumped down on a stool beside Miles. "Morning."

"So our boy is leaving us for a spell," Dad informed, pride tugging at the corners of his mouth. "He's going off to chase his dreams. Leaving his poor mama back here brokenhearted," he teased.

Miles grinned. "If she has her way, I'll be forty and still living in the basement."

"Isn't that the truth?" Dad chuckled, his eyes gleaming.

"What's this about forty and living in the basement?" Mom's voice sang out as she entered the kitchen.

Ellie followed at her heels, dragging her blanket behind her. Groggy and still fighting with the dream fairies, a nagging whine bleated from her.

"I wanted to sleep a little longer."

"Ellie, you can't. Mommy has a full day today, and you need to go to play school." Mom said.

"No," she whimpered.

I bent and scooped her up.

"Hush all that fussing, Ellie. No one wants to listen to your whining this early in the morning," I scolded, pressing my nose against her. "You got that, young lady?"

"Jules, you can stay home. Maybe you can be sick with one of your bad head pains?" she suggested, halting her whining.

I curbed a giggle at her innocent suggestion. But our family wasn't so tactful in concealing their smirking faces.

"Yeah, no, I'll pass on a migraine, Ellie."

I set her down on the stool beside me. "Ellie, do you want some yogurt with frozen berries for breakfast?" I asked.

She nodded.

I glanced at Mom who breathed a, "Thank you."

I responded with a half-smile, trotting to the fridge to retrieve the ingredients for Ellie's breakfast.

"Valentine's day is coming up, Jewel. What do you and Kaiden have planned?" Mom questioned, handing me a bowl.

"I don't know. He says some things need to be a secret." I smiled. Popping a strawberry in my mouth, I remembered Kaiden's smug face when I inquired about where we would be going.

"Well, it looks like Miles will be babysitting Ellie. Because I'm also taking this exotic beauty out." Dad seized Mom around the waist and twirled her into his arms.

"Quinn." She giggled. Interest piquing, she asked, "Where are we going?"

"It's a secret." Dad's eyes twinkled.

"Oh, you." She pounded his chest lightly with her fist.

Miles looked down at Ellie, who stood by his chair smiling at the display of affection between our parents.

"Well, Ellie, if it's just me and you, what do you want to do?"

Her cheeks turned a shade of pink, and she said, "Surprise me."

"What?" Miles jaw hung open. "Am I missing something? We have two women right here saying they hate surprises. Then we have a four-year-old saying surprise me? You women are confusing." Turning to Dad, he said, "You see why I don't need one, right, Dad? I am the sane one, after all. Point proven. Thank you all very much." Jutting his hands in the air, he peered toward the ceiling.

We laughed at his antics.

"I'm five," Ellie notified Miles. Clearly, he had left her behind at that part of his conversation.

The kitchen erupted with laughter.

My tires skid on the layer of black ice beneath the new covering of snow, forcing me to drive at a slower pace and delaying my arrival in picking up Amy. As I pulled into Amy's street, my heart sunk at the sight of flashing lights ahead.

As I edged closer to Amy's house, my palms began to sweat. My knuckles whitened and gripped the steering wheel. Realization submerged a sickness in my stomach when I saw an ambulance parked in her driveway. Two cop cars blocked her driveway. A fire truck sat across the street. Neighbors perched on their steps, wondering what was happening. Various people in uniforms swarmed the front yard.

*What the heck is going on?*

On the opposite side of the street, I slowed my car to a stop.

The front door opened and two paramedics pulling a stretcher exited. On the stretcher was a black body bag. Amy's parents followed after the paramedics. As the paramedics lifted the stretcher down the front steps, Mrs. Kent buried her face into her husband's shoulder. He leaned into her, and they appeared to be weeping.

Stunned, I glanced at the body bag and then back to the Kents. I raised a hand to my throat. I couldn't breathe, an invisible hand choked the air from my lungs as grief overshadowed me.

I knew it was Amy in the bag. I clambered from my car. Leaving the door ajar, I fled across the street and up to the Kent's, weaving in and out of the crowd. Hands pulled at me, begging me to stop. Frantically, I clawed them away. I stumbled onto the front steps as I reached Amy's parents.

"Amy? What happened?" I beseeched them.

Mrs. Kent, surprised at my appearance, lifted her head from her husband's shoulder. Their faces were as white as the flurries falling around us. Mrs. Kent's eyes were red-rimmed and swollen. Momentarily, she peered at me before returning to the comfort of her husband's embrace.

My eyes darted to the evidently deep and profound grief that governed the face of Amy's father.

"She, um …" He cleared his throat. "We found her … she was hanging in her closet."

"What? No, it has to be a mistake. We just talked about this," I insisted. "I mean, she didn't mean to. She couldn't have—" I broke off.

"She left a note," he said, the wetness of his eyes mauling at me.

"No, no, no, no," I screamed, racing to catch up with the paramedics. "Stop, please stop," I begged.

They did.

"She can't breathe. Unzip that bag," I demanded.

A glimmer of pity and anguish crossed their faces. They looked past me to the Kents. I turned to look at them too. Mr. Kent nodded to the paramedic.

One of them unzipped the black bag. I edged forward, demanding my weakening legs to do their part.

I saw the blueish, tinged face peeking out of the bag. I didn't stop. I moved on. I had to see for myself. Stopping at the side of the stretcher, I peered down at the face laying within. Her luscious red hair hung loose, framing her face. The burns of a rope marred her slender neck. Her eyes were closed, and her thick auburn lashes kissed her cheeks. In death, her face displayed a grimace, mocking the hardship of her young life. I touched her cheek, and her skin was cool to my touch.

Violent sobs racked my body as her name escaped my lips. "Amy … I'm … I'm sorry." I sobbed, my hands cramped into fists as I grabbed at the body bag.

"Mom … Dad … Kaiden, someone, please." I groaned as

my knees gave way, and I crumpled into a heap on the frigid ground.

"Miss, is there someone we can call?" a male voice asked. I felt the stranger's hands guide me to my feet.

"I need to get out of here," I wailed, peering around trying to gain my bearings. I glanced up at the man who held me. It was an officer. I peeled myself from his grasp. Slipping and sliding on the ice, I ran toward my car.

My keys slipped from my hand and tumbled to the ground. God help me. My soul screamed out. Someone placed gentle hands on my shoulders.

I stopped. Leaning my head against the roof of my car, I wept. I sobbed for the girl whose life had been smudged out. Her youth stolen from her. They'd pushed her too far. I cried for the loss of the girl who'd given me a chance.

Taking a deep breath to settle myself, I turned to find the salt and pepper haired police officer who had previously tried to console me.

How did they do this? Day in and day out seeing the monstrosities in the world. Waking up every day and going to work knowing this was what they might encounter.

His eyes reflected the emotions gripping at him with the loss of an innocent life.

"You know this is the direct result of bullying," I said with immotile conviction. "For some of us, going to school is like walking to our own crucifixion. We are told we need an education, but when we are there, we can barely function and get through the day. We don't know what lies around the next corner. We fear who is waiting for us at our locker, or in the bathroom, or in some dark corner of the school. How about when you're sitting in a classroom and it's your year to get the shitty teacher? The one who decides to make you her project of making herself feel better. Teachers are put in a position to educate us and encourage us, but some target students, saying things a teacher should never say." I let out the years of pent-up grievances of the injustice I suffered.

The officer lifted a hand to scratch his face, and his eyes dropped.

"Yes, that's right. Even in our honorable school system, there are crappy teachers who breed self-loathing in their students." Mentally, I was done. I wanted to run and keep running. Far from everyone and everything. To a new world where everything was perfect. "I'm … I'm sorry, Officer. It's just that no one hears our voices. She …" I turned to watch the ambulance drive away. The flashing lights had been turned off because Amy's life was no longer an emergency. Her face would no longer brighten my day. She was no more. "She fought to simply exist. In a place we have no choice but to attend if we wish to succeed."

No more words formed in my head as I stared up at him.

Tears welling in his eyes, he stated, "You shouldn't be driving. We should call your parents."

"I'm good. I live five minutes from here." I lied.

He hesitated before stepping back. "All right, straight home."

I nodded.

On the drive home, his final words to me reeled in my head.

"Let the devastation of this day help you change the outcome for others. Be a voice in the dark. Find a purpose in this."

# CHAPTER TWENTY-FOUR

*Kaiden*

My heart plunged at the sound of the deep-seated sorrow that coated her voice when she called to tell me of Amy's suicide. A glance at the speedometer to confirm my speeding. My foot lumbering on the gas pedal in my urgency to get to her. Like an addict coming down from a high, my hands shook on the steering wheel

My tires squealed to a halt outside her house. Turning off the engine, I sprinted to the front door. Seconds after I rang the doorbell, Mrs. Hart opened the door. She should've been at the office by now. But it was evident in her puffy eyes, Amy's suicide rattled everyone.

Silently, she stepped back.

Inside, I closed the door behind me.

"Kaiden." Jewel's cry echoed from above.

I glanced up into the open hallway of the second floor. She stood at the railing, peering down at me.

"Jewel." I looked at Mrs. Hart, who nodded her permission, and then I took the stairs two at a time.

At the top of the stairs, she crumpled into my arms.

"She is gone, Kai. Amy is gone." She burst into hysterics.

"I know, Beauty. I know." I soothed her, stroking her hair.

The doorbell rang. Mrs. Hart answered the door, the wind blew a scattering of snow across the floor. The snowstorm brewing outside had picked up its pace.

On the other side of the door stood Finn and his mom. Finn's usual neatly managed hair was disheveled. He stood with his hands shoved deep into his jean pockets.

"Hi, are Jewel and Kaiden here?" His voice trembled.

"Yes, come in."

We hurried down the stairs as they stepped inside, and Mrs. Hart closed the door behind them.

Finn stood unmoving. He stared blankly at us as we approached.

"Hey, Finn," Jewel said.

He didn't speak. Tremors resonated through his body as he continued to stare.

"Finn? Maybe you should take a seat," I suggested.

"Yes, come sit down, Finn," Mrs. Hart urged.

In the living room, I led him to the couch. Jewel and I sat down on either side of him. The silence was intense and oppressing. My ears tuned into the humming of the dishwasher in the next room.

Minutes passed before Finn broke the silence.

"Where do we go from here?" he asked, never lifting his eyes from the coffee table he'd glued them to.

Jewel looked at me.

"We'll figure it out, Finn," I said.

I wanted to comfort him, but what could I say when I was unsure myself? A girl, our friend, had taken her own life. The girl he was still head over heels in love with. No more would her footsteps sound on this earth.

"We will figure it out," Jewel attempted to assure him.

"You all have each other. That is the support you need to lean on," Finn's mom added.

Mrs. Hart nodded and smiled softly down at us. "Yes, Mrs. Gracia is right. Amy would want that."

They wanted to say the right thing, but somehow, it seemed inadequate. Life would go on. I suppose it always did. Things would never be the same. Bullying had robbed her of life. Her cry for help had fallen on deaf ears. We didn't think she would take her life. But had we not been aware of all the threats and attacks on her? I couldn't help but feel we failed her in some way.

"I'll make us some tea," Mrs. Hart said to Mrs. Gracia.

We sat for hours talking about Amy and the good she'd brought to our lives. Maybe Jewel and Finn's moms were right. We did have each other. Together we would find a way to climb out of the despair entangling us.

## Jewel

Amy's funeral took place a few days later, and the turnout was in the hundreds. Finn, Kaiden, and I sat in our pew surrounded by our families. As people filed into the church, a song playing over the speakers stirred in my ears. I recognized the song as "Dancing in the Sky." In reverence, I closed my eyes and whispered a wish up to Amy.

*I hope you are dancing, Amy. No more pain, no more heartache.*

Fighting back the tears, I felt Kaiden's fingers interlock with mine. Opening my eyes, I glanced at him and saw his eyes brimmed with tears. Snuggling into his side, I laid my head on his shoulder. He pulled me closer, and the warmth of our touch provided the comfort we sought. I questioned God. Why would he give me a friend to only take her away? The cruelty of it all remained beyond my understanding. What had Amy's purpose been in life? I thought back to Amy's last words, "Thanks, Jewel, for being my friend." Her words were her final goodbye to me. Maybe in time, I could forgive myself for the blame burrowing in me. Maybe, if I'd clued in, I could've saved her. I brushed away the nagging thoughts marring my mind.

Raising my eyes toward heaven, I whispered to myself, "The honor was truly mine, my friend."

The oxygen became obstructed in my lungs. Lexi and Jess sat down a few pews in front of us. I observed the people around me. Mr. B sat off to the left with his head bowed low. I scanned over the backs of the other teachers and principal. My eyes settled on the imposter.

Mrs. Barker?

My fingernails dug into my palm. My eyes charred holes through the back of her leopard print blouse. How dare she dishonor Amy like this? Amy had gone to her about the attacks from Lexi and Jess, but she'd turned her away. Mrs. Barker should be ashamed to face Amy's family and friends, yet here she sat, warming a pew.

My attention turned back to Lexi and Jess. Jess stared straight ahead, but the slumped shoulders of Lexi caused me to pause. The side profile of her face revealed a face with no makeup. Never have I seen her without a perfectly sculpted face. Her face appeared puffy and drawn from crying. Could it be Lexi finally cared? I hoped guilt ate at her because she had done this. Lexi and Jess might as well have put the noose around Amy's neck. How would they ever live with themselves? Jess was disconnected from the world, that was obvious, but that was her norm. It was as if emotions never existed in her. But Lexi? Presently, I watched as she struggled with her inner emotions, and at this moment, I wanted her to choke on them.

I narrowed my focus to the oversized picture positioned at the front of the church beside Amy's closed casket. The girl in the picture illuminated beauty and happiness. She'd fought to survive, but in the end, the pain won out. She would never graduate or go on to college. Never marry and have children. She would've been a great mom. Always so loving and kind. I missed her, and the loss of her grew suffocating.

The beautiful service ended, and the guests made their way out of the church. They mingled in the parking lot and paid their respects to the Kents. I made my way to Amy's parents to offer my condolences. In an attempt to get through this grueling day, they nodded and smiled.

Mrs. Kent's eyes touched mine, and her set smile softened. It wasn't Amy's intent to cause them this pain. She loved them. But when you are hurting so bad inside, you aren't thinking of others. You just want it to end. In her pain, she never thought of her loved ones. The ones who were left picking up the pieces.

I reached out a hand to touch Mrs. Kent's. "I have no words to make this okay. I only wanted you to know how much Amy helped change my life."

"Thank you, Jewel. Thank you for being a friend to our girl," Mrs. Kent replied sadly.

"I only wish we hadn't taken so long to find each other," I replied.

"Me too." Her voice fractured with tears.

Mr. Kent retrieved an envelope from his pocket. Handing it to me, he said, "I believe she left you a letter too."

"What?" I glanced at my name she'd scribbled across the front of the envelope. Tracing the letters with the tips of my finger, I lifted my eyes to look at her parents as my tears began to flow.

"Thank you," I mumbled.

Amy's been gone for days. The understanding she wasn't coming back was settling in. It was midnight and a hush had befallen my house. Miserable and sleepless, I toss and turn in the transparent shadowy darkness invading my room. The moonlit night shone through the crack in my curtains. Willowy long claws form on my walls from the branches of the red maples outside.

Turning on my side and facing the wall, I thought of Kaiden. He'd been calling and texting, but I couldn't face him. The inner battle I fight tormented my every waking thought. When I slept, I dreamed of her. The same dream over and over. I couldn't stand it. Was I going insane?

In my dreams, she visited me. *She's sitting on a bench in a beautiful park. The sky cloudless and the sun achingly bright.*

*Each time, I jog up to her and call her name. She doesn't turn; it's as if she doesn't hear me. Her hair gleams bright and alluring under the sun's blaze. It hangs loose, covering her face, and as I draw near, her sobs circulate in my ears. My heart clenches, and I rub my sweaty palms on my pants. I sit down on the bench beside her. Lifting a hand, I try to tuck her hair back. She turns to me, and I scream lurching back. Her face is hollowed and empty without any features, but she starts to groan. At first, I can't understand what she is saying, it comes out muffled. I strain to grasp her words. I have to understand them. Something in me is begging for her words to set me free. When the words become clear, I began to cry, and then I'm floating. Her words grow louder and louder, "You knew, you knew." Her wail becomes desperate.*

*I cry out to her. "I didn't, Amy. I didn't. I'm sorry."*

I woke up crying, and each night, I dreamed the same dream again. Guilt viciously gnarled at me because I wanted to tell someone. But would they blame me too? As I lay here, I tried to muzzle the negative thoughts spinning in my head. I thought of happy thoughts, like our Christmas break in New Orleans.

Then I hear her. A replay of that dark year of my life. Her footsteps pausing outside my door before she tiptoed across my carpet.

Mom.

I closed my eyes. I didn't want her to know I was awake. As she drew near, she held her breath. Reaching out, she pressed her fingers to my wrist and checked for my pulse, then blew out a calming breath. She whispered a few words. A prayer?

As she brushed back the hair cascading over my cheek,

I felt her kiss my forehead and she whispered, "I love you, sweet girl." Like a thief in the night, she tiptoed back out. I listened to her light footsteps wander down the hall to her room.

I weeped for the worry and agony that tortured her. I wanted to tell her about the never-ending rhythmic torment that was killing me, but I didn't.

## Lexi

"Mom, where are you?" Lexi yelled as she walked into the living room. "Mom!"

She wandered down the hallway to her mother's room and opened the door. "Mom!" she cried, turning away to avoid the view of her naked mother with her new flavor of the week.

"Lexi! What are you doing home?"

"I live here, what do you think. I didn't realize I needed to inform you of coming into my own house." Lexi looked back at her and her twenty-something old boy toy.

"Probably last night's bartender," she grumbled to herself.

"Watch your mouth," her mom said as she shuffled out of bed and put on a bathrobe. "Here sweetheart, put this on." She threw him Lexi's dad's robe.

Lexi's eyes pierced through the side of her mother's head as she turned and walked away. She ambled out to the couch and sat down. She peered at her trembling hands, and she placed them under her thighs in an effort to stop the tremors. She felt tired all the time lately and she now had to wear a belt with most of her pants.

She winced as the image of Amy's face popped into head.

"No, no, no," she mumbled and pressed her hands to her face. Tears stung her eyes.

*What have I done? What have I done? I want to take it back. Please let me take it back. I'm sorry.*

"What now, Lexi?" her mom said, strolling into the living room.

Lexi opened her hands to look at her mom. Wiping the tears from her eyes, she made an attempt to smooth her tangled hair.

Lexi peered at her with a deadly stare.

Why couldn't she have been the one to leave? Maybe with Dad here, I wouldn't have turned out like this. I hated her and myself.

"I needed advice."

Her mom laughed as she walked into the kitchen and meandered over to the liquor cabinet and pulled down a bottle of tequila. She threw the cap on the counter, and Lexi watched as it rolled to the edge and dropped. Her mom came to sit beside her on the couch. She chugged back a big drink and turned her diluted pupils to her. "Since when do you come looking for advice from me?" She grunted. "We both know you hate me, and I can't say the feeling isn't mutual."

Lexi dropped her eyes. No matter how many times her mother said things like this, it didn't hurt any less and her tears resurfaced.

Her mother threw back another big gulp and used the back of her hand to wipe her mouth. "Here, looks like you could use this." She shoved the bottle at her.

Lexi didn't move. Her mom thumped the bottle against the side of her arm. "It isn't going to get any better. Any fool can see guilt is eating you up over that girl you killed."

Lexi's eyes whipped up to meet hers, and her mom smiled at the effect of her words. "That isn't the only thing you should feel guilty about. You know as much as I do that you're responsible for your dad leaving," she spat, dropping the bottle in Lexi's lap and hauling herself off the couch.

Lexi stared at the bottle long after she was gone.

"What's the use?" She shrugged her shoulders and lifted the bottle to her lips and gulped one drink followed by another and another.

# CHAPTER TWENTY-FIVE

*Kaiden*

Weeks had passed, and we were forever changed by Amy's suicide. Finn could become solemn and angry all in the same breath. Jewel withdrew into herself. She ignored my calls and texts. We are falling apart.

Alone. I felt like I was drowning. I needed them to throw me a lifeline, but it never came. If I wanted it to change, I had to make it happen myself. She would see me, and I wouldn't leave until she did. I couldn't take much more of this. I needed her.

A shiver went through me as I stood on the front step of her home. Mrs. Hart answered the door, "Kaiden? Hello …" Dark circles had formed under her eyes.

"Hello, Mrs. Hart. Is Jewel home?"

She smiled, and her eyes grew watery. "Yes, she is. She hasn't wanted to see anyone, but I don't think it's the best thing anymore. Come inside out of the cold." She took me by the arm.

I stepped inside, and she softly closed the door behind me.

"She is in her room. Please forgive her. She is hurting and can't move out of her own head to realize you and Finn are hurting too." Mrs. Hart's brushed at the desolate tears moistening her eyes.

I coughed over the lump in my throat. I lifted a hand and tenderly stroked her shoulder. "It will be okay, Mrs. Hart. She will come through this. We will help her together," I assured.

"Yes, we have to. We must. What the Kents are going through, I can't begin to comprehend. We've been there with Jewel. This could've been us burying, my baby—" Sobs depleted her voice.

"Mrs. Hart, please … " I wasn't sure what to do. Her tears suppressed my breathing. Stepping forward, I wrapped her in my arms. For a brief span of time, I cradled the mom of the girl I loved. When her sobs tapered off, I let her go.

"Thank you, Kaiden." She raised a trembling hand and wiped again at her cheeks. "You've been the best thing for Jewel, and she needs you now as much as you need her. Why don't you go on up." She patted my arm, and a beautiful smile emitted on her face.

From upstairs, I glanced back down at the main floor at Mrs. Hart. She stood with her arms wrapped snuggly around herself as she paced. Jewel had a support system which was epic at a time like this, and I was determined to do my part in reviving her back to the bubbly, outgoing girl I knew.

At her room, I found her door open. She wasn't closing out the world around her, and this gave me hope. In my mom's bad days, she often closed her door to retreat into her own reality and to push everyone away, including me. I peeked inside and found Jewel sitting at her sketching desk. Her recently brushed, thick, glossy hair lay free and flowing down her back. She wore oversized black sweatpants and a bright pink long-sleeve jersey shirt. Her shoulders were slumped forward, and the pencil in her hand laid short even strokes on the paper in front of her.

I knocked on the doorframe.

Startled at my intrusion, she spun, dropping her pencil. "Kai … I didn't. I wasn't expecting you," she sputtered.

"I know, but I've been trying to reach you for over a week," I asserted firmly.

"Yes, about that." She dropped her head, and her shoulders hunched forward.

"I know you miss her. We all do." I pleaded all too aware of the loss she was feeling.

"Come, sit with me." She moved to sit crossed legged in the center of the bed.

I lowered myself on the edge of the bed. The mixed emotions stewing in me rose as I looked at her. "We needed you. I needed you. Don't you understand that? We are all suffering, but you abandoned Finn and me—"

"Kaiden?"

"No, Jewel, we all lost her. Are you going to pine away in this room while the rest of us worry about you and try to find the strength to go on ourselves." I stood and started pacing the room, pouring out my jumbled thoughts. "I won't be part of it. I can't go through this again. You need to pull yourself together. Your mother is down there pacing the floor and dying inside with worry over you. Please, Jewel, don't shut us out. If not for us, do it for Amy. Honor her memory."

Her body stiffened, and her eyes bore into me. "This is exactly why I didn't say anything. You think I'm playing the victim. I'm not the victim. We all are. Yes, my soul is tormented. I was the last one she spoke to before she died. I could have stopped it. She would still be alive if I had clued into her last words. I blame Lexi and Jess, but I may as well have put the rope around her neck myself. The night before she died, she thanked me." A feverishness controlled the hands she lifted, yanking at her hair.

"Thanked you?" I asked.

"Yes, I called her. Her last words were, 'Thank you, Jewel, for being a good friend to me.' She told me how tired she was. I didn't think she was in the headspace to take her own life. I was aware she'd struggled with thoughts of suicide, but I thought she was past it. I wish I would have known. I would have gone to her place or had her come here. I wish—"

"Stop it, Jewel! I don't want to hear another word of you blaming yourself," I demanded "How could you have ever known? You were a better friend to Amy than anyone ever was. She wouldn't want this. Us falling apart and blaming ourselves for not seeing the signs. She thanked you! She wanted you to know how much she cared for you and what you had done for her. We can't let her death go as another disturbed teen. She needs to be remembered for the good she was." I went to sit on the bed beside her.

"Why are you always the voice of reason? " she said dryly, tilting her head to look at me. "You're always so strong."

I calmed my pounding heart and regarded my clasped hands in my lap before peering at her. "I'm tired of being the strong one."

Her eyes softened, and she laid her hands over mine. The warmth of her hands made me long to hold her in my arms. Long to shut out the world and be lost in the bliss of each other's arms.

"I'm sorry, Kaiden. I failed you and Finn. I know it's no excuse. But a case of self-blame and resentment got the best of me."

"I get it, Jewel. I don't want to fight with you, but I need you to want to live again. We have to go on. Life is about the ups and downs. But together life doesn't seem so unbearable."

Jewel studied me intensely, and a bright smile encased her face. She rocked forward on her knees and threw her arms around my neck.

"You are amazing, " she breathed in my ear as she kissed a trail of sweet kisses down my jaw, and her lips met mine. Hungrily, I covered hers in a feverish urgency.

"Well. Maybe I should inform Mom of the make-out session going on in here."

I broke away from Jewel with a whole other urgency. I spun to find Miles leaning against the doorframe.

Jewel soured at her brother, sending him a glare. "Miles!" She tossed a pillow at him.

He grinned and ducked as the pillow whipped past his head.

I smirked at her display of sisterly love.

"Hey, Kaiden, how are you?" Miles asked.

"I'm doing okay. Thanks."

"Well, it's good to see you got this one from adding any more permanent grooves into that bed. Now, if you could get her out of her room, it wouldn't smell so funky in here." His eyes cinched with mine.

Jewel hissed her annoyance at him.

I read the meaning behind his keen eyes. I knew him to be the kind of guy who didn't get too concerned by much. But now, his eyes silently pleaded with me to help his sister. He straightened, bid us goodbye, and ambled down the hall.

I sat quietly staring at the empty doorway.

"Kai?" Jewel's voice drew my attention.

I looked at her. "Yes?"

"You okay?"

"Yes, I'm fine."

Her eyes wandered over my face, her soft hand caressing my cheek. "Thank you for not giving up on me."

Hope surged within me. There was a renewed light surfacing in her eyes. There she was. The girl who took on the world like a trooper.

"I think you should get out of the house. What do you say?"

"I don't know, Kai," she said hesitantly.

"It will do you some good to have a change of scenery," I urged.

"Maybe you're right. Give me thirty minutes, okay?"

"I'll ask Finn if he wants to join us."

"That would be nice. I hope he isn't too disappointed by my disappearance." She bit her lower lip.

"He cares about you. If he is mad, he will get over it," I said with a small smile.

"I hope so. Now out, so I can get ready." She giggled, giving me a shove.

I laughed and placed a peck on her forehead before strutting from the room.

# Jewel

The fog muddling my brain parted, revealing an inkling of my old self. As I readied for a confirmed night out with Finn and Kaiden, I thought long and hard about the choices I would apply to my life from here on out. Kaiden's word scored profoundly in my mind. He needed me… Finn and my family, they all needed me. I needed to pull myself up out of the tidal waves I'd condemned myself to. I had allowed my grief and guilt to sweep me away from what mattered in life.

"Jewel?" Mom called.

"In here," I yelled out from the chaise in my closet.

She poked her head inside as I buttoned the last button on my smoky gray short-sleeve top.

"Hey, honey. Kaiden said you were going out?" She held her breath.

"Yes, we are."

"That makes me extremely happy," she said, clasping her hands under her chin.

I returned her smile. "Me too."

"In time, the pain won't be so crippling."

I yearned for everything to be all right again, but I knew it never would. "That's what I hold on to," I replied.

"The loss of Amy is extremely hard for you all. Take her death and turn it into a positive. Tell her story. Don't let the world forget her. Tell anyone one who will listen. Get them to truly absorb the impact that malicious, mean words and actions can take on a life. As women, we are emotional creatures. Because it's the makeup of our design. We are like flowers. If you don't water and nurture a flower, the petals began to fall, and without realizing it, the flower shrivels up and dies. Like us, each nasty and condescending remark we throw at each other peels away at who we are ... until, like Amy, we fade away."

Her words captivated my broken soul and struck a chord deep in me. I could hear Amy's sweet, melodious voice call out to me.

*Live.*

I contrived myself to heed the voice as hers instead of my own subconscious urging me to fight.

My heart rejoiced as I looked up at the woman who was always there in the shadows. Even when she didn't know I was aware of it.

"I'm going to fight this. I will spend a lifetime remembering her," I said with more certainty and clarity than I'd had in almost two weeks.

"Good," Mom cheered. Straightening, she turned to leave.

"Mom."

"Yes?" She paused and twisted to glance back.

"I will be stronger. You don't have to worry anymore."

"Honey, I'm a mother. It's my job to worry." She laughed.

"I mean at night. Sleep. I will still be here in the morning. I promise."

Her eyes widened and recognition dawned on her face. She silently nodded and turned and drifted out the door. My heart overflowed with love for her, and a hum fell from my lips as I finished getting ready.

# CHAPTER TWENTY-SIX

*Jewel*

The peacefulness of the ranch called to me more frequently over the next month. Riding Cherish across the expanding countryside with the whisking of the wind on my face gave me a sense of being alive and helped restore a new disposition in me.

After my ride at the ranch today, I would be dropping by the Kents. I hadn't seen them since the funeral. This morning, I called Mrs. Kent to ask about paying her a visit. She sounded delighted by the idea. Over the past six weeks, they'd been on my mind, but fear kept me from contacting them. What if they weren't ready to see me? What if the sight of me was only a reminder of what they had lost.

On my way to the Kents, I made a quick stop at the bakery. Amy and I often stopped by to grab her mom's favorite pastries.

Driving up the Kent's street set in motion the screenplay

of that tragic morning. I shook my head to push the images away. Parking my car in the driveway, I gathered the pastries and lattes I'd purchased.

Ringing the doorbell, I glanced back at my car, starting to question my decision on getting the pastries. But before I could return them, the door swung open.

*Crap.*

"Hello, Mrs. Kent." My voice came out like a squeak.

"Hello, sweetheart," she greeted, her eyes targeting the box of pastries.

She centered her eyes back on mine, a smile tipping the corner of her mouth. "You've got a powerful grip on those pastries; is it because you're not looking to share?"

I blew out a breath of relief. Smiling, I pressed the box toward her welcoming hands.

"She made me stop for these a time or two. I know they're your favorite."

Her eyes dampened. "I've been craving these heavenly delights, but I couldn't muster the courage to go to the bakery." She rubbed her thumbs over the box like it was a precious gift. "Oh, my goodness. Where are my manners? Come in."

Seated in the kitchen, I looked at Amy's mom. Overall, she seemed to be faring well. But her eyes were tired and sad.

"I'm glad you called, Jewel. Amy used to keep this house lively. Now, it seems dull and lifeless. I don't think it will ever be the same," she said, peering down into her cup of tea.

"I understand. Amy put the joy into a conversation, and she added a whole lot of sass when she wanted to state her opinion." I giggled.

Mrs. Kent's head whipped up, and she chuckled. "A sass

to go with those amazing red locks of hers."

"Finn believed her to be the best thing he'd ever set his sights on. I remember the day she sat down beside him in the cafeteria. I thought I'd have to ask the janitor for a mop to wipe the drool off the floor." I smiled at the memory.

A deep belly chuckle came from Mrs. Kent. She shook her head and dabbed the tears from her eyes. "Oh, I remember when her head started to swarm with affections for Mr. Gracia. Finn this and Finn that. I started to get Finned out."

"Honestly?" I asked, raising a brow. "I mean. I knew she cared about him, but I wasn't sure how much."

"Yes, he's the first young man she fully trusted. He was patient and kind, and that drew her to him. Amy had a rough start in life, and though I thought we'd given her everything, I wanted so badly to be the perfect family. To provide Amy with a life that would expunge her past. In the desire to achieve this, I know now I failed my daughter. I blocked out what she was trying to say to me. I didn't want to believe she was being bullied, so I painted it over in my mind as silly girl jealousy that would fade. I never stopped to listen to the pain she was in. I mean, I knew she used to self-harm, but I thought it had stopped. I fooled myself into believing she had it all so there was no way she would still feel the need. I never educated myself on the reasons for self-harm until it was too late." A shudder coursed through her.

"We all have regrets, Mrs. Kent, but I'm learning it does none of us any good. The good we can do is remember her for the special person she was. The guys and I thought of ideas to raise awareness about teen suicide and bullying. Right here in our community. I wondered if maybe you and Mr. Kent wanted to team up with us? We've requested the school board give us permission to speak at the schools around the Toronto area. What do you say? Would you be interested?"

"Yes, yes," she cheered clapping her hands together, bringing them to her lips.

"Great." I grinned.

A while later, she hugged me goodbye and thanked me for giving her something to hold on to. Our conversation inspired me on the steps we would take to make a difference in the lives of the kids we could reach.

On the way home, with my radio cranked, I tapped my fingers against my steering wheel as I belted out the song it played.

March faded into April and spring sprang early, temperatures for the end of April hitting a record high. As graduation drew near, the senior class's focus turned to the preparation of prom night. Kaiden and I tread lightly around the topic of prom with Finn. Finn had planned to attend with Amy.

We'd contemplated asking Finn about his plan for prom for weeks now because the timing never seemed quite right. But today I would ask and hope for the best. The three of us sat at the picnic tables outside at lunch hour.

"I know it's not something you want to talk about, Finn, but we want you to come to prom with us," I said.

"Umm, I don't know about that," he said.

"It wouldn't be the same without you, Finn," Kaiden added.

"Look, I appreciate the consideration, but I'm not looking

to be the third wheel." Finn directed his gaze from Kaiden to me. "I'm not sure I would feel right about going without her."

"I get it, Finn. We both fight those same feelings. But she wouldn't want us to sit home and miss our prom," I urged with a smile.

"You're probably right. It would seem weird. But I will give it some thought." His gaze traveled beyond us.

"That's all we ask," Kaiden assured.

"Perfect," I said with a grin.

My attention drifted to Lexi as she stumbled around the corner of the school. Leaning her forehead against the building to steady herself, she appeared to be intoxicated again. This had become the new Lexi since Amy's death. A few times too many, she'd shown up at school reeking of booze. Her eyes bloodshot and her clothing looking like they'd been slept in.

Jess and Chad came tracking behind her. Chad's arm hung around Jess's shoulder. Lexi, oblivious to her surroundings, didn't see the kiss Chad brazenly planted on Jess's mouth.

I wasn't sure why that irked me so bad, but it did. Lexi's fall from grace had been Jess's rise to queen bee of the school. The whole matter sickened me. Chad leaned in and said something to Lexi before he and Jess paraded off. After their departure, Lexi slumped against the wall.

"Will you two excuse me?" I said and strolled toward Lexi.

As I drew near, her distress became certain. Her knees trembled, and she grasped at the wall to keep from falling. I reached out to steady her. Not hearing my approach, she flinched.

"What, now?" she cried, turning her swollen, disoriented gaze to me. "Jewel? What do you want?"

"You don't look so hot, Lexi."

"What do you care? No one cares," she said, devoid of emotion.

Was I supposed to care about someone who'd caused me nothing but pain? What was I doing here anyway? I hadn't quite figured it out. Something drew me to her now. But with her whining, I wanted to drop her where she stood. The sound of her voice was bad enough, but her whining was grating.

"You need to sit down," I said, helping her to the ground.

Okay, now turn and walk away. Nope, I didn't. I sat down beside her.

I sat for a moment beside my enemy. Thinking of the girl she helped send to her grave.

"Why are you here, Jewel? I thought I'd be the last one you would care about."

"You are," I replied, grimly. She tensed beside me. "You've never been kind to me, and you don't deserve my kindness now. But there has been enough pain. You need help, Lexi."

"Oh, here we go," she mocked. "Remember the last time you tried to help me?" She laughed bitterly before dropping her eyes to her hands resting in her lap. Her body shuddered and a long sigh came from her. In her wasted muddled brain, she was absorbing what I'd said.

"You're right. I need help."

We sat in silence for a few seconds more.

"Jewel?"

"Yeah?"

"I'm sorry."

I held my breath as she said the words I'd needed to hear

for so long.

"I was ashamed and humiliated because you spoke the truth. To cover up my embarrassment, I went after you. I was wrong for that and so many other things. I'm sorry. I know nothing I say can change the hurt I've caused you."

I wanted to scream at her and drive it deep into her skull—the damage she had caused, not only to me but also to Amy—but I said, "It's about what you do now that will prove you are sorry. We've lost one girl this year, and you are headed down the same road. Make the right choice and choose life. You can't change what's been done, but you can change what you choose to do from here on out."

I spotted Kaiden and Finn strolling toward us, and I stood.

She glanced up at me, tears veiled her eyes. She didn't speak because what words could she say? She acknowledged my words with a nod.

I sauntered off to meet the guys.

"What was that all about?" a perplexed, Kaiden asked.

"I hope you told her what a piece of scum she is," Finn muttered.

"What is the use? Would it make us any better than her?"

"What? Now you are going to act superior? Like you're Mother Teresa, all giving and gracious? " Finn said hotly.

"Finn!" Kaiden brows dipped.

"Okay, I know. Look, I'm sorry, Jewel. I don't mean to lash out at you, but it peeves me off. She is looking to take the easy way out by drinking and numbing the guilt. I want her to feel it. I want the guilt and pain we are all dealing with to slap her full on in the face. But as usual, she is taking the wrong way out."

"The difference between her and us, Finn, is she is alone. We have the support of each other." I stopped and glanced back at Lexi. She sat with her knees drawn up to her chest and her face buried in them.

Compassion and empathy rose in me for the girl who'd played a part in taking Amy from us. A girl who drove me to a place I almost didn't come back from. Now, she sat begging someone to care and for someone to lead her back from the treacherous path she had started down.

# CHAPTER TWENTY-SEVEN

*Jewel*

My final dress fitting arrived. The dream of going to my prom always seemed unattainable. A mixture of emotions mauled at me as Mom pulled open the glass door that read, "Amore Designer Dresses." Though the thought of dancing the night away in Kaiden's arms seemed magical, this appointment had been made for Amy and I, and a hardness dropped in the pit of my stomach as we walked through the doors.

"Welcome to Amore Designer Dresses," greeted the owner, Madam Amélie, who sauntered in from the back room.

"Ahh, Natalia, mon chéri. You're glamorous and regal as always," charmed the well-preserved lady of around sixty years of age. She kissed Mom's cheek then the other. Stepping back, she raised a jeweled hand, smoothing her cinnamon feathery-fine hair.

"Madam Amélie, always a pleasure." A smile quenched Mom's face.

Madam Amélie turned her over-the-top charm on me, and I blushed under her praise. "Jewel, your youth and beauty are an inspiration." She took my hand and twirled me around for her inspection. "Perfection," she purred, her extra-long false lashes brushing the top of her rouge-dusted cheeks. "I have your dress hanging in the dressing room. Whenever you are ready, you can head back. Natalia, let me get you a glass of champagne. We have some lovely white chocolate-covered strawberries freshly brought in this afternoon."

I excused myself and headed to the dressing room. The room was small but lavishly decorated. Black and silver damask wallpaper covered the walls. A button tailored ivory chair sat in the corner, and a grand oversized chandelier was the focal point of the room. I pulled the embroidered silver curtain closed behind me.

Eager to see if my hard work at losing five pounds before this dress fitting would pay off, I wiggled out of my clothes. I unzipped the white garment bag, revealing the backless red silk gown within.

I slipped the halter style dress over my head. The dress was unforgiving, but as the material slid over my body, and the length dropped to brush the floor, I was ecstatic with the results of my determination. The fabric lay smooth and flattering against my body. My heart soared with happiness.

Never had I felt this beautiful.

I twirled in the floor-length mirror, inspecting the back. The backless dress plunged into a deep v that stopped at the base of my hips. A few days in the sun and Mom's lemon olive oil sugar scrub would achieve the dewy summer glow I would need to pull off this dress. If only I'd spent some time toning my arms and not solely focused on flattening my stomach.

"How is it going in there?" Madam Amélie's voice snapped me out of my scrutinizing.

"Good, I'm coming out," I called back. Pulling back the curtain, I exited the changing room.

Madam Amélie's eyes widened as she lifted a hand to her overly large half-exposed breasts.

"Oh, mon Dieu! Exquis!"

The blood rushed to my cheeks at her fuss.

"I say we go and show ta Maman. What do you say?"

"Yes." I gave her a smile.

The gold speckled white quartz tile was cold under my feet as we ambled to the mirrored sitting room. Mom gasped as I rounded the corner, and a hand leaped to her mouth. Her eyes clouded with the proud mom waterworks.

"Oh, Jewel, you are simply breathtaking. That body, my lord. Oh, to be young again." She bubbled looking at Madam Amélie in wonderment.

"Tell me about it. All these girls come in here hating their bodies. But as grown women, we drool over the desire to have back the bodies of our youth." Madam Amélie huffed.

Mom stifled a laugh, "Isn't that the truth."

"All right, Jewel, step up on the platform, and I will check if we need to make any further adjustments."

I ascended the one step circular platform and turned to look in the 360-degree mirrors.

I peered at the image of myself with appreciation. My shoulders were drawn back and my chin tucked upward. Happiness lurched from my eyes.

This past year was a simple glimpse at what life had in

store for me. I was beginning to find purpose. Why life waited so long to give me a chance was still a mystery. Why I had to struggle with the trials sent my way, I still couldn't put my finger on it. How many years had I spent trying to hurry my life along in the desire to be done with school and away from my peers? But lately, I found myself sad and maybe a little scared of what the future held. I wanted to pump the brakes at becoming an adult. Was the adult world not ten times as scary?

"Jewel, my God, you are so beautiful," Mom reiterated again as she came to stand by me.

"Thanks, Mom," I beamed as I smoothed my hips with my hands.

She handed me my white diamond sparkled three-inch heels. I slipped them on my feet, wobbling a bit as I adjusted to the thin heels. I'd marched for weeks around the house in these shoes, trying to learn how to walk in them. My toes pinched, but I'd suffer the pain for this one night.

I left the store wishing I could fast forward time to prom night.

## Lexi

Jewel's words kept Lexi awake at night. Her effort to care when she owed Lexi nothing weighed on her. Hadn't she found pleasure in seeing Jewel's pain? If Jewel was more alone, then Lexi felt people would focus on her and not the hopeless mess she was.

As she pulled into the school parking lot a few weeks later, Jewels words, "It's what you do now that matters," echoed in her head yet again. What could she do differently? She had no one. No adults in her life would help her. Her mother cared only about herself and held on to some twisted hope her dad would come running back to her. Lexi was alone in the world, and she needed to learn to deal with that. If no one else cared, why should she?

"Morning," Eric called out in passing as she stepped out of her car.

"Oh, hi Eric," she said, hurrying to catch up with him.

He took a quick look at her, and his eyebrows lowered. "Lexi, you need to get it together."

She shot him a glare. "Excuse me?"

"You look like shit."

"Screw off, Eric." She jutted her chin and glowered at him as she twisted to walk away.

He grabbed her arm. "Hold on before you go stomping off with your nose bent out of shape."

She jerked to free her arm, but he held on tight. She struggled for a moment longer before she gave in and stood still.

"Are you going to hear me out?"

"Yes," she said through gritted teeth.

"Good. I don't mean to offend you, Lexi. You got dealt a crappy life, but a lot of us have. Everyone has their own issues, but if you aren't going to fight for yourself, who will? You can either deal with the mess in your head or you can end up a drunk with absolutely nothing. The path you are headed down will only lead to more pain."

His outlook on her future chilled her. A drunk like her mom. No way. She wanted nothing more than to be as far away from the woman as possible. The last thing she wanted was to be anything like her. Every moment she looked at Chad, she began to hate him more. Why couldn't she have been attracted to someone like Eric?

"But how, Eric? How do I start to pull myself out of this cocoon I've formed around me?" Her eyes searched his.

"I can't answer that, Lexi. But you have good in you somewhere. We all do. It comes down to the choices we make. Maybe start by making different choices." He gave her shoulder a light pat before he turned and jogged across the lawn to the school.

She watched him go. Like Jewel, he was right. She could blame it on Jewel's perfect life as the reason for Jewel making the choices she did. But what of Eric? His life wasn't perfect. His dad had run off too, yet he still held himself together.

Her heart was heavy as she walked into the school. She was at her locker when the speaker screeched and a voice rumbled over it.

"Lexi Clark to the office."

What now? She slammed her locker shut and snapped her lock on. With a spin of the dial, she trotted off to the office.

She strolled up to the secretary.

"Hi, you called me."

"Yes, Mr. Pepper requested to see you in his office. Please take a seat until he says the announcements."

Seconds later, Mr. Peppers voice echoed over the speaker.

"Please rise for the Canadian anthem."

She stood at attention as the song played out. After the morning announcements, Mr. Pepper came to get her. The door to his office was open, and she sucked in a breath when she saw Mr. and Mrs. Kent seated inside.

What did they want? Her heart thumped with force.

"Please take a seat, Lexi," Mr. Pepper said, gesturing at an empty chair a few feet from the Kents.

She wiped her clammy hands on her leggings as she took a seat. Her body jerked and twitched as she raised her eyes to look at Amy's parents. She hadn't seen them since the funeral. What could they want?

"Lexi, I'm sure you know the Kents." Mr. Pepper said.

"Yes," her voice whispered.

"We spoke to your mother and asked her to be here for this. She said she was tied up but gave us her permission to speak to you on this matter."

Of course, she was tied up. Why wouldn't she be?

"What matter?" she asked, glancing from him to the Kents.

Tears formed in Mr. Kent's eyes, and his chin quivered. Lexi choked back the restriction in her throat at the emotion she saw on his face. Her eyes flickered to Mrs. Kent, and she was taken aback by the soft smile that played on her lips.

"Lexi, we asked you here today because we have something that we would like to discuss with you." Mrs. Kent twisted her hands in her lap before going on. "Please know we aren't here to point fingers. Our girl is gone, but you are still here. We want to be a glimmer of light in your life. We failed Amy, but maybe by offering our help to you, we can somehow make it right."

"W- what do you mean?" she asked, her foot tapping rapidly beneath her chair.

"I've spoken to your mother."

"You did?"

"Yes, she was none too kind when she threw me out of

your house. She refused to allow me to help you, but Mr. Pepper did call her and was able to convince her to let you get the help you need."

"What are you referring to?" Lexi pulled at her leggings as she adjusted herself in her seat.

It was so hot in here. Her throat scratched and begged for water.

"We would like to send you to a wellness retreat."

"A wellness retreat? Like a place for crazy people?" she retorted as she looked at Mr. Pepper.

He raised his hand. "Lexi, hear them out."

She clamped her lips shut and circled her eyes back to the Kents. "Go on."

"This isn't a place for crazy people. It's a place for people who are hurting. A place to heal and deal with the things which caused you to make the choices you have. It's too late for Amy, but it's not for you. I have one request of you, Lexi, and that is to be a voice in this world. Yes, you may have done wrong. Yes, maybe you've hurt people, but you too are hurting. You need to fix you, and in doing so, you can turn your life around. You can change. I believe with the right help and people in your corner, you can make a difference. Don't throw your life away. Break the chains of dysfunction in your life."

Lexi wrapped her arms around herself as tears streamed down her cheeks.

How could they show her this much compassion? She had taken their daughter from them. She didn't deserve their kindness.

"I … I don't know what to say." She used the sleeve of her hoodie to wipe her tears.

"Say yes! Yes, I choose me. Yes, I choose life." Mr. Kent

spoke for the first time.

Lexi broke and buried her face in her arms and wept. She heard movement and then the warmth of tender arms surrounded her.

"You are worthy," Mrs. Kent whispered in her ear.

Fifteen minutes later, she exited the office, gathered her books, and left the school. She needed time to think. She'd taken the Kents offer and agreed to go to treatment. Prom was a week away, and it was agreed she would go the following day. Others would be going off to college and university while she clung to the hope it wasn't too late for her. For the first time in years, she believed something good was in store.

# CHAPTER TWENTY-EIGHT

*Kaiden*

From the back of the limo, I clutched the plastic container holding Jewel's corsage. Gently, I stroked a thumb over the top of the closed lid. I'd chosen her favorite flowers. White orchids with a touch of greenery and berries accenting the pearl bracelet corsage.

To say I was excited to see her would downplay my enthusiasm. I thought about how she'd taunted me with a bat of her lashes and the glide of her hand over my chest. She'd tantalized my senses with a scant description of what her dress looked like. My polished black laced shoes drummed on the floor of the limo as the driver inched toward her street.

Before leaving home, Mom blinded me with the flashing of her camera. As the limo pulled away, she let me know she would meet me at the Hart's, where the endless photos would continue. I'd laughed at the excitement covering her face. The months spent with my grandparents helped Mom become the healthier version I remembered before the loss of my dad. This alone made the future look brighter. Life now held nothing but promises.

The limo rolled to a stop outside her house. Through the tinted windows, I saw Mom waiting in her car. When the driver opened the door, I slid out and nodded my thanks. Straightening, I adjusted the buttons on my tux jacket.

My mom came to meet me, and taking her hand, I tucked it in the crease of my elbow.

Her eyes gleamed as she gazed up at me, a slight pinch between her brows puzzled me.

"What is it, Mom?"

"You look like him."

"Huh?" I frowned at her.

"Your dad. You look like him on our prom night."

I gulped at her words.

"But you may be a tad bit more handsome as you have my genes too," she teased with an extra squeeze to my arm.

I laughed.

"I'm so proud of you, Kaiden. Going off to university. You need to be away from all the pain and burdens you have dealt with over the past few years. I'm getting better, and I can do this on my own. Besides, I know you will be in good hands with a certain blonde," she said with a wink.

"Thanks, Mom."

I loved her, and seeing the glow of good health in her face made my heart rest easy with my recent acceptance into the University of Calgary. I lifted her fingers to my lips and kissed them.

Mr. Hart opened the door as we ascended the front steps.

"Kaiden, Sarah, please come in," he greeted us with a

charming smile and a sweep of his arm.

Mrs. Hart wandered into the foyer followed by the pandering feet of Ellie.

"Kaiden!" Ellie squeaked, running across the marble tiles to get to me. I bent down to her level and embraced her in a gentle hug.

"Hey, Ellie."

In her excitement of the evening, she squeezed me extra tight around the neck.

"You look like your getting married." She giggled as she pulled back to inspect me. "But Jules doesn't. Her dress is a long red dress, and you can't wear red to get married," she said matter-of-factly before pointing at the corsage in my hand. "Is that her flower?"

"Yes, it's for her wrist," I added with a smirk of amusement at the pint-size girl full of opinions before me.

"I know that part. She has a flower for your coat too. I've been watching it all day in the fridge, making sure it stays perfect for Jules's night," she beamed.

"How kind of you, Ellie," I said and looked past her to the three grinning adults.

"Kaiden, you look so handsome." Mrs. Hart smiled at me.

"Thanks."

"If I didn't know you to be the man you are, Kaiden, I'd have to sit you down and go over the rules of my daughter's safe return." Mr. Hart's eyes teased.

"Quinn, behave," Mrs. Hart chirped at him.

Mom laughed at the exchange of banter between the two.

The sound of Jewel's shoes on the dark hardwood drew our attention to the spiraling staircase. Breathing deeply, I turned to soak in the view of my prom date, catching sight of the bottom of her red silk dress and a flash of her open-toed diamond shoes. She clutched the material of her dress as she descended the stairs.

My breath caught and the world stood still for the red enchanter who intoxicated me in her spell.

"Wow," I whispered as she took the last step.

I gulped back the thickening in my throat. I admired how the dress slid over her body. Half of her hair was pinned up and half lay in soft curls dangling down her back.

My eyes moved to her face, and the glint in her eyes said it all. Happiness exuded from her and quickened my heart. She meekly turned for us to see the back. My heart skipped a beat as she swirled, revealing the deep-cut open back. The desire to hold her in my arms and cover her body with kisses compelled me to drop my gaze.

I was unnerved by the passion pumping through my veins in the presence of her parents.

"Kaiden, give her the corsage," Mom said, cutting through my trance.

I sputtered and forced my feet to move to the girl who had to be a dream. How could it be that this vision of perfection was my date?

Her eyes danced with delight as they scanned over me. "Kai, you look amazing." She entwined her hand in mine. Her hand was soft and stirred the feelings I was trying to contain.

"You don't look so shabby yourself." I stumbled like a blabbering idiot.

She lifted a brow.

I cleared my throat. "I could say you are beautiful, but somehow, the word falls flat beside the vision you are."

She laughed, lifting her chin. "I think, I will take that as a compliment."

My shaking hands could be heard as I struggled to open the plastic container to retrieve the corsage within.

Jewel laughed, holding out a hand. "Let me help you with that."

Why was she so damn calm? Wasn't I usually the calm one? I had put so much emphasis on making this night perfect for her, and now I was screwing it up.

"Please do."

Effortlessly, she opened it and held it out to me. I withdrew the corsage and slipped it onto her wrist.

"All right, picture time," Mom coaxed.

Turning to face our families, I slipped an arm around Jewel's waist. As my hand glided over her exposed lower back, an electrical current surged through us. I felt her shiver. I didn't dare look at her, and I avoided Mr. Hart's eyes like the plague.

"Smile," our moms singsonged.

The next ten minutes seemed like hours as we appeased our parents with the memories they required. The muscles in my jaw ached from the effort it required.

"Well, we will let you two get out of here," Mr. Hart chimed.

I was thankful for his understanding of our moms' overkill.

I clasped my hand in Jewel's, and we hurried to escape the watchful eye of our parents. In the limo, she wasted no time sealing her lips to mine. My hand slid around her back, pulling her body to me. She raised her arms, locking them around my neck.

Moments later, I summoned up some restraint and broke our embrace. Our eyes entangled with feverish desire. Lifting a finger, she wiped her red lipstick from my lips. Settling back against the seat, she linked her fingers with mine.

I grinned at her. "Off to share you with your other prom date."

She laughed, moving in closer to me. "Yes, it's a rare occasion that I am in such high demand."

Wrapping my arm around her shoulder, I caressed her satiny smooth skin. The scent of her wild cherry blossom shampoo threatened to be the undoing of me.

*You're killing me.*

## Jewel

The flashing frenzy of the mom paparazzi at Finn's house appeared to be in full effect. Finn was bent into a pose on the front step when we arrived. His dark hair and complexion were striking against his crisp white tuxedo. A red pocket handkerchief peeked out of his front breast pocket.

Kaiden slipped his hand in mine as we strolled up the walk to greet him. Eagerly, he waved at us, more than happy to be done with his modeling gig.

"You look like a blond Latina," Finn said. Taking my hand, he twirled me around. "I hope you are ready to tear up the dance floor?"

"Thanks, Finn. You look dapper yourself. I may be a disappointment in the dancing department. Just a heads-up."

A boyish smile charmed his face. "It's all good."

Kaiden handed me Finn's boutonniere, and I pinned it

on the lapel on his jacket. "There," I said with a pat of my hand on his chest.

Another round of photos took place before we were on our way to the school.

The parking lot was lined with limos dropping off grads and their dates. Excitement echoed in the evening breeze as the students filed toward the school. From lavish ball gowns to trumpet style dresses, girls were accented with crystals and diamonds that blinked and glittered in their splendor.

"What do you guys say we grace the doors of this place one last time?" I glanced from one date to the other.

They nodded, each offering me an arm. I happily looped a hand in the crook of their arms.

On one arm stood my boyfriend, and on the other stood my friend.

I closed my eyes and thought of her.

*This one's for you, Amy.*

"Ready?" Kaiden asked, smiling down at me.

"Yes," I said, giving his arm a gentle squeeze. Covering my hand with his, he started toward the front entrance.

When we walked out these doors tonight, we would be leaving here as adults in an unsure world and no longer students. Trading our youth with the hopes and dreams of a bright future.

Music drifted toward us as we opened the main doors. The corridor leading to the gymnasium was decorated in black and white streamers with matching balloons. The decorating team brilliantly pulled off our theme, A Night in Paris.

Entering the gym, we strolled down the cobblestone runner walkway. Black post streetlights lit and lined the walkway. Hundreds of white streaming lights hung from the ceiling.

A giant black Eiffel Tower surrounded with glistening white lights stood off to the right. A few smaller towers strategically placed throughout the room. In the center of the gym hung a massive chandelier, casting a romantic glow in the dimmed gym lights. White and gold balloons hung in low clusters from the ceiling and surrounded the floor in front of the refreshment tables.

We stared in wonderment and awe at the transformation of the gym.

"Wow, the design students outdid themselves," Finn praised, looking around.

"It actually is like a night in Paris." I smiled.

"He must be the new principal." Kaiden nudged his head toward a man dressed in a fine tailored gray suit who appeared to be in his late thirties. He stood speaking to a few teachers while his eyes traveled over the grads.

"Let's hope the fresh blood will do this school some good," I said.

"What could Mr. Pepper do but resign after another suicide this year? He was too laid back about things that mattered. At least he showed some remorse," Finn added.

"Well, my mom and Mrs. Kent haven't stopped and will continue making a difference here in our community after we go off to university in the fall. Even though they can't seem to get anywhere with the school board, I think with media awareness and the work they are doing around the schools and even at this school, things can't stay the same," I said with a sense of pride. "I can't believe Mrs. Barker hasn't been let go. That is the one thing that eats at me. Maybe Mr. Dress Sharp will finally give her, her walking papers."

"We can't change everything, but at least we are making

progress," Finn said.

"This is true." I smiled.

The band began a new song. My fingers involuntarily tapped Kaiden's arm to the beat of the music.

"Not to abandon you all, but I see Mr. B over there, and I thought I may slip off and pick his brain for a bit," Finn said.

"Sure, whatever works. But remember, Finn, to let that brain of yours rest some and enjoy this night," Kaiden suggested.

"I promise. I will," Finn said, raising his hands to the sides of his hair and smoothing it back. A smirk covered his face as he glided back into a moonwalk before dramatically twisting on his heels and sauntering off to bombard Mr. B with his questions.

"Now, Beauty, I get you all to myself." Kaiden's husky whisper in my ear sent a heated sensation through me.

I turned to him and withdrew playfully from his grip.

"Don't forget I have two dates tonight." I held up two manicured fingers. He reached out and snatched them down.

"I call first dibs on the first dance."

"Oh, shucks. But I already promised Finn the first dance."

"Sure, you did." His eyes danced as I slipped my hand into his. The warmth and security of his grip charged my heart with completeness. I pressed a kiss to his cheek before whispering the words he had waited to hear.

"I love you, Kaiden Carter."

His eyes widened, and he shouted, "Finally!"

Heat crept into my cheeks as his shout drew the attention of the students around us.

He swept me out the doors of the gym to a shadowed corner in the darkened hallway. The passion running untamed through my body blanketed the chill of the wall. Kaiden leaned into me, resting an arm against the wall over my head. With his free hand, he lifted my chin and placed a soft peck on my lips, my cheek, and the tip of my earlobe, and then his mouth wandered down the curve of my neck.

"Kai …" I whispered.

"Yes," his sexy voice whispered back.

Pressing my hands against his chest, I drew back so I could look into his eyes.

"Thank you for taking me to our prom and giving me a memorable high school experience."

He rested his hands on either side of my hips, and his words scored my soul.

"This is what you deserve, Jewel, and much more. Who would have thought we would meet in our senior year. You gave me purpose and hope for what life could be outside the pressures of my bleak life at home. You've been the good in my life."

"There you two are."

"Hey, Finn," I said.

"Well, you promised me a dance and I'm here to collect." He grinned.

I laughed and linked my arm with his.

"Then, let me go make a fool of us."

"Gracia, you are lucky I like you. Trying to steal my girl and the first dance." Kaiden snorted.

"Well, you had your opportunity, but instead, you decided to come out here for a make-out session. Besides, if she had looked my way years ago, she wouldn't be yours now," Finn mused.

# CHAPTER TWENTY-NINE

*Jewel*

I n Finn's arms, I danced our first dance of the night. His
Latino dance skills left me breathless as we sailed around
the dance floor. A sheen of happiness gleamed in his face,
and it buoyed my hope that we were going to be all right. Each
day, we healed a little more, and each day, we were learning
how to move on.

Finn twirled me from one corner of the room to another.
My eyes scanned the room for Kaiden. I found him standing
off to the side of the beverage table. One hand was casually
tucked in his pants pocket and he held a glass of punch to his
lips. His eyes followed me, and when our gaze met, he tilted
his glass in a cheer.

A warm song of joy and fulfillment flowed through me.
Selflessly, he stood waiting with no jealousy or animosity as
his friend held his girlfriend in his arms for what should've
been our first dance. He loved and cared for people with his

whole heart. At this moment, he was the sexiest I'd ever seen him. I loved the way he loved me. He was my all.

Finn shouted at me over the music. "You know I can envision you two married before you are out of vet school."

I reflected my attention back to my dance partner. "Who knows what the future holds. I want to live it, one day at a time, and see where it takes us."

Finn looked past me, resting his gaze on Kaiden. "He brings out the best in you, Jewel. Never have you shone as much as you have this year."

"He kind of has that effect on people." I grinned in appreciation as the song was coming to an end.

"He is a pretty great guy; I'm going to have to agree. He's been a good friend to me."

"You and me both. Like you and Amy ..." I flinched as her name dropped from my mouth. "I'm sorry, Finn. I didn't mean to bring up her name."

"It's all right. She deserves to be celebrated."

We turned to glance at the picture of Amy. A tribute to the grad whose tassel would not be turned at commencement. The grad whose laughter and excitement of a future would not dazzle this room tonight.

"We had some fun times. Didn't we?"

"Yes, we did." A solo tear slid from the corner of his eye.

"We all—"

Someone banged into me from behind, and I stumbled. My knees buckled, and my ankle twisted. I grabbed at Finn as I fell to my knees. Immediate throbbing pain shot through me.

"For God's sake, watch out, Jewel," Chad grumbled.

Finn glared up at him as he kneeled beside me.

"Chad? I believe it was you who weren't watching where you were going."

"Shut up, Gracia."

Chad reached down and jerked me to my feet. He smelled bathed in alcohol. Instead of releasing me, he pulled me close. His hot breath burned as he rubbed his nose up the side of my neck. He inhaled like I was a satisfying drug.

"Stop it. You're drunk," I seethed.

He snorted. One of his hands held me prisoner while the other slid down to my butt and squeezed.

"Firm and delectable like I imagined."

"Screw off, Chad, and let go of me." I pounded at his chest while trying to break free from his drunken grasp. His sweaty hand on the bare flesh of my back sent shivers up and down my spine. I slapped his face, but in his drunken state, it never fazed him.

"Chad, release her now!" Fire charging from his eyes, Finn pushed at the overpowering muscle mass who held me.

The dancing around us stopped as students paused to take in the scene unfolding. All hell broke loose when Kaiden seized Chad's collar from behind. Chad let out a yelp of shock, releasing me and sending me tumbling into Finn.

"Let go of her, you bastard!" Kaiden bellowed, his eyes dark and dangerous.

"What's it to you, Carter?" Chad sneered, sizing Kaiden up.

My lip quivered at his crass outburst, but I never moved my eyes from them. Mortified, I stood without moving. Never had I seen Kaiden like this. He grabbed the front of Chad's shirt and drew back, his fist ready to find its mark.

Finn grabbed Kaiden as Eric and Jess arrived and

attempted to cool Chad down.

"All right, break it up." Mr. B's voice intervened as he pushed his way through the crowd. "Kaiden, release him," he ordered.

Kaiden obeyed, but his eyes scorched their warning at Chad.

Mr. B directed his attention to Chad. "Chad, what is your role in all this?"

"I did nothing. We ran into each other, and she fell."

"It wasn't the running into her that was the issue, Mr. B. It's the piggish behavior he treated her with. Like she is a piece of meat he can put his filthy hands all over." Finn snarled.

Kaiden's nostrils flared, and the hardness amplified in his dark eyes.

Limping to stand beside him, I reached for his hand.

"Jewel, is this the truth?" Mr. B asked. "Did Chad behave inappropriately toward you?"

I turned to Mr. B. "Yes, Chad seems to think he can speak to girls in whatever vulgar manner he wants and he groped me like I was his possession." My eyes flashed from the pompous ass jock to Mr. B. Mr. B's face turned a dark shade of purple, and he swiveled back to Chad. "All right, that's it. Mr. Palmer, you will be escorted out of this event."

"But—" Chad started to protest.

"Not a word. You're done." Mr. B took Chad by the arm.

"But Mr. B, it's prom night," Jess started to protest.

"Not a word out of you, Jessica. I suggest you find a new date as Mr. Palmer will be heading home." He turned and escorted Chad out of the gym.

"Good job, Jewel. Thanks for ruining the evening." Jess glared.

"Don't blame me for Chad's actions." I returned her glare.

With a stomp of her heels, she stormed off.

"Are you all right?" Kaiden's gaze shifted to me.

"Yes, I will be fine. But I'm going to have to go barefoot for the rest of the evening as I twisted my ankle and can't wear these heels." I held on to Kaiden's arm and bent down to remove my shoes. My toes immediately thanking me.

Finn shook his head in bewilderment. "Did you smell the booze on him?"

"Yes, he reeked of it," I said.

"I think I'll get a drink of straight up punch. You guys want any?" Finn asked.

"Yes, I'll take one, please."

"I'm good," Kaiden said sourly.

"Okay, I'll catch you later," Finn said, spinning on his heels, and he was gone.

"Let's go have a look at your ankle," Kaiden said, leading me to the side of the gym where a row of chairs had been placed.

He lifted my ankle to investigate the damage.

"There doesn't appear to be any swelling," he said as he gently rubbed my ankle.

"No matter what Chad does or says, he can't ruin this evening."

"You're right; let me go find some ice for your ankle."

Minutes after he left, a shadow fell over me, and I glanced up to find Lexi.

"Are you all right?" she asked.

She was stunning in a slim-fitting long teal dress. A slit ran three-quarters of the way up her leg. Her makeup was flawless, and her eyes appeared to be clear.

"Yes."

Silence stilled the air between us.

"Good." She turned to leave but halted. Turning back, she said, "You look amazing, by the way." A half-smile curved her mouth.

I speculated for a moment where she had hidden her evil twin because this girl standing in front of me was not Lexi.

"Thank you. I think? You look good too."

"I wanted you to know I've taken your advice about getting help, and I'm going away for a while to a wellness retreat. I've been messed up for a long time. Maybe I'll never get better; I don't know. But your words have played in my head, and for some reason, no matter how much I try to subdue them with alcohol,, they are still there. Eric, he has been a good friend to me lately. He is more than I deserve. I don't know if he even likes me as a person or if he is just being Eric."

I couldn't find the words to speak and offered her a small smile.

"Anyway, I do wish you the best in life, Jewel, and if I could change what I've done to you, I would. If I can tell you one thing, it would be, it was never you, it was all me," she said with a sad smile before she turned and walked away.

Tears blurred my vision.

Friendship would never be in our future, but I needed to give credit where credit was due. She had made an effort to offer an olive branch, and that had to stand for something.

Hours later, as the evening drew to a close and the grads

started to dwindle, Finn, Kaiden and I decided to call it a night. Exhilaration vibrated through me as we walked through the corridor and out the front door.

High school would now be part of our past, and like my friends, I was more than happy for that. I would be going off to vet school in the fall. Kaiden and Finn were also accepted at the University of Calgary. Kaiden would be studying psychology. Finn, on the other hand, was offered scholarships from the university and would be going for his bachelor of science.

My hand sealed in Kaiden's as our feet touched the pavement of the parking lot. Kaiden and Finn joked and carried on. I smiled at their ribbing. Friends for a lifetime had been our pledge.

Then it happened.

Our heads jerked up as the oncoming blinding white headlights raced toward us.

"Jewel," Kaiden cried, his panicked hands shoving me with such force, I flew toward the sidewalk. I screamed as I hit the pavement, and my arm became pinned under me and snapped. Searing pain radiated throughout my body as the asphalt tore at my flesh. But it was the sound of squealing tires and the car hitting someone that resonated and paralyzed my brain.

No, no, no. Please, no.

I struggled to rise. I had to get to them. My stomach dropped as my eyes fell on Finn in the amber glare of the headlights. He was kneeling over the silhouette of a body which lay motionless on the ground.

Kaiden? No, no. It can't be.

A shrill scream shook the night deafening me. I lifted my

hands to my ears to block out the scream. My fingers trembled with the vibrating in my head. I recognized the scream as my own. Pain emanated through my arm, and I dropped it to my side. I pushed myself in his direction. Lead confined my legs, and it seemed like I was treading on air.

I reached him as the stunned driver exited the car.

"Kaiden!" I screamed, dropping to my knees beside him. As I pushed back his hair, a wetness dripped through my fingers. Lifting my hand, the headlights revealed the crimson liquid trickling down my hand.

Blood? Oh, no, God no. My panic heightened and nausea charged through me. I clawed at my chest, trying to rid the blood from my hand. No, this wasn't happening.

Finn sprang into action and retrieved his cell phone from his pocket.

He shouted into the phone, "Yes, hello, there's been an accident at York Mill Composite High School."

Kaiden. Wake up. Please wake up.

I wanted to lift him and hold him in my arms, but I knew I couldn't. I leaned closer and kissed his forehead. His blood moistened my lips and a wail gripped my throat. "Hold on, Kai. Please don't leave me. I need you." Tears shed from my eyes and dropped on his face. I rested my cheek on his. "Please Kai, I'm begging you. Hold on. Please hold on." An utter sense of loss and despair overtook me. "You promised you wouldn't leave me behind. You promised."

I was unaware of the shadow of the human profile towering over me until he spoke.

"I … I didn't mean to. I didn't see him," the driver pleaded.

Chad? My mind placed the voice. A match struck in me

as I glared up at the drunken fool in front of me.

"If he dies, you will pay. I promise you this, Chad Palmer. No amount of money will save you from paying for this."

Finn wrapped an arm around my quivering shoulders and took Kaiden's hand in his.

"Hang in there, buddy, they're coming. It's going to be all right."

There was so much blood. How could this be okay? I was going to lose him. He was my backbone, my strength, my friend. He couldn't die. He couldn't. I could not live without him. I wouldn't live without him. Moments ago, I had it all. Now I sat covered in the blood of my boyfriend, unsure if he was going to die.

My eyes blurred as sorrow pierced me. "Don't let him die, Finn. Please don't let him die. We can't lose him. We can't lose anyone else."

"I know, Jewel. I know." He choked on a sob.

The sound of the ambulance drew near.

"Jewel, Finn. My God, what happened." Mr. B's voice cut through the night.

I turned to find Lexi and Mr. B running toward us. Mr. B dropped to his knees beside me and a groan came from him.

"He is hurt bad, Mr. B." I sobbed.

His eyes were grim as he looked at me.

"I didn't see them. I swear," Chad cried.

Mr. B's eyes shot up at him. "Chad!" he bellowed. "What are you still doing here? I put your ass in a cab and sent you home."

Chad's shoulders quaked with rising panic. "I messed up. I—"

"You did this?" Lexi shrieked. "You're drunk, and you got

behind the wheel?"

My head snapped in her direction. Lexi now stood in front of him.

"I ... I—"

"No." She shook her finger in his face. "No, excuses Chad. If he dies, it's all over for you. How could you be so stupid?"

He did not reply. His eyes dashed around as flashing lights came into view.

"His mom. We have to call his mom," Finn cried.

"Yes, I didn't think," I said. Finn handed me his phone, and with trembling fingers, I searched for her name and pressed the call button.

Kaiden's mom's sleep induced voice came over the phone, "Hello."

"Mrs. Carter, there has been ... an accident," I whispered.

# CHAPTER THIRTY

*Jewel*

T he craze in the emergency room was disorienting. I stood powerless watching the paramedics as they rushed Kaiden's stretcher down the corridor and out of my sight.

In a daze and numb of emotions, I glanced around the emergency room uncertain what to do. Most of the blue-gray cushioned chairs were taken. People openly stared at me. A sick baby screamed at the top of its lungs before phlegm choked off its cries. A man held a blood-drenched cloth around his forearm. The beeping of machines and the non-stop ringing of the phones blared like sirens. The room began to spin as panic and anxiety wrenched through me. I needed to wake up from this nightmare. I must wake up.

Someone placed a hand on my back. In the muddiness controlling my brain, I peered at the blurred faces of Finn and Mr. B. Their mouths were moving, but their words went inaudible. I turned to gaze at the person standing beside me whose hand tried to ease my agony.

Lexi? What is she doing here?

Her fingers burned like a branding iron on my back, and I shirked from her touch.

"Jewel. Where is he?" I gave heed to the panicked voice of Mrs. Carter. Turning, I viewed her and Kaiden's grandparents rushing toward me. As their penetrating eyes raked over me, their impending worry intensified mine.

I didn't speak. I wanted to. I opened my mouth, but no words came out.

"Jewel, please, I need to know where my son is," his mom begged, grabbing me roughly in her urgency. Pain surged through my injured arm, and I cried out.

"They took him back there." I pointed down the corridor. "On the way, I heard them say something about possible brain injury. He saved my life. He pushed me out of the way."

Mrs. Carter's eyes widened, and as I spoke the words, the horror of this night became real. Kaiden was back there somewhere fighting for his life all because a drunk driver made the egotistical choice to get behind the wheel.

Mrs. Carter spun on her heels and went to speak to one of the nurses behind the desk. Mr. B and Kaiden's grandparents followed after her.

"You need to have your arm checked out," Finn was saying.

"Okay." I fiercely shook my head. "But I need to be here when they come back. I have to know what is happening."

"All right, please sit down at least. You look ready to collapse. I'll tell the nurse."

Not long after, the ER doctor checked me out and

ordered me to be sent for an X-ray. Finn guided me to a chair to wait for the X-ray as my parents sprinted through the sliding glass doors of the emergency entrance.

What were they doing here? Did I call them?

"I called them. Mr. B thought you needed them," Finn said.

I frowned at his reply. Hadn't I said that to myself?

"Jewel!" Mom cried as her distraught eyes came to rest on me. They once again hastened their steps, and Mom promptly kneeled to examine me. "Are you hurt?"

"No, I'm fine." My eyes blurred with a torrent of fresh tears.

"Mom, I can't lose him. I can't," I pleaded with her.

Her warm hands embraced mine. "I know, honey. Kaiden is a fighter. Don't give up hope."

Dad's hand moved to my face, and the crust of Kaiden's dried blood crumbled under the stroke of his thumb. His blue eyes dampened as his hand cupped my cheek. Seeing the worry etched in his eyes, I felt the color drain from my face. I wiped my clammy hands on my blood-stained dress. He didn't worry often, and the look in his eyes sent my anxiety racing.

I glanced over at Mr. B standing at the desk beside Mrs. Carter. His hand resting on her shoulder as he looked from Mrs. Carter to the cherry-red haired nurse behind the desk. Mrs. Carter was talking rapidly, her hands waving in the air as she spoke.

Soon, Mrs. Carter returned with Mr. B.

"What did they say?" I asked.

Mrs. Carter's face was drawn and tight. "He is having a CT scan. They aren't giving much information without the consult of the doctor. So now we play the waiting game. How did this even happen?"

"Chad was drunk. Mr. B sent him home in a taxi earlier, but he must've driven his car back to the school," Finn said.

"Where is he now?" Mrs. Carter eyes narrowed.

"Last we saw him, the cops were leading him away in handcuffs," Lexi said, a shudder jolting through her body.

I looked at her and noted the tears streaming down her face.

"What? You miss that piece of trash, already?" I exploded. Why was she even here? Why wasn't she running after her stupid boyfriend?

"No … it's not that," Lexi said.

"Then, why?"

"Because of our selfish ways we've caused so much pain. Lives are forever changed because we are so screwed up in the head," she replied, her shoulders sagging as her eyes met mine. "I'm to blame for Amy. I understand that. Not a day goes by when I don't live with regret, and Chad, who knows what life has for him now. So many ruined lives, and for what reason?"

"You are to blame. You got that damn right," I spewed, and the bitterness I held toward her reared its ugly head. "You may as well have killed her yourself. You stole her from us. Just like your disgusting boyfriend may take Kaiden from us."

"Jewel, that's enough," Dad scolded.

"Why, Dad? She's caused me years of pain, so why should I spare her feelings?" I said, burying him in my wrath.

He gestured toward Lexi. "Because the girl standing here is hurting too."

The pain in my chest was as if he'd plunged a knife into my chest.

"Traitor!" I screamed. Jumping to my feet, I dash toward the exit, ignoring Mom as she called after me.

I couldn't breathe. Desperate for air, I sprinted through the doors and into the night. The drizzle of rain pattered down on my tear soaked cheeks.

Traitor. Traitor. How could he defend her?

Finding a dark corner by a hedge of bushes, I leaned back against the brick wall of the hospital. Grief ruptured through my body like a torrent as I looked up into the bleak, starless sky.

Why? Everything was perfect. "Why?" I screamed at the greater being we were often told of.

The chill of this miserable night laid claim to my weakening legs, and I slid down the wall. I curled my knees to my chest and sobbed for the gazillionth time that night. The rain began to come down in sheets. Its hushed but relentless pelting washed away my tears in the streams trickling across the pavement.

Someone slid down beside me and gently settled their arm over my shoulders. The pain of my arm jarred me, ceasing my sobs.

"Don't give up hope, Jewel," Finn said as he tenderly pulled me into his embrace. I gave in to the comfort of my friend, and the pressure of his arm didn't resonate as much.

"I was mean, wasn't I?" I muffled into his shoulder.

"You are hurting and scared. Trust me, they understand," he reassured.

I sighed. "I will apologize. But right now, I can't."

He kissed the top of my head. "Lexi left anyway. It doesn't

change the way she's been for years or what she's done, but it appears she has remorse. Hopefully, she won't do anything stupid. There's been enough suffering."

I nodded into his shoulder.

I knew he was right.

The flow of people through the hospital's sliding glass doors was constant. Their pain-filled faces resonated the dread, amplifying in me with each agonizing minute.

Hours crept by as we waited in the congested emergency room. I wondered about the battery life of the outdated oak clock that sat cockeyed on the cool mint green walls. I stared at the bright white cast that now bound my arm.

Every time a doctor or someone with a clipboard entered the room, we froze. Were they the one who would ease or heighten our worries? A doctor dressed in green scrubs wandered into the room. Several sets of eyes pinned on him in anticipation. We waited to see who would be called and given the news of their loved one.

"Kaiden Carter," he said, glancing around for the persons who would respond.

"Yes," Mrs. Carter called out. Clutching her purse to her side, she hurried to speak with him. Kaiden's grandfather took his wife's hand in his and followed their daughter.

I sat on the edge of my seat. The fingers on my good hand dug into the man-made leather that covered it. Vigilantly, I watched Kaiden's family until the doctor guided them down the corridor and out of my view.

A soft whimper expelled from me.

"We'll get news soon," Mom said with a stroke of a hand on my back.

Breathe.

Ten minutes later, the Carters reappeared. Smiles enveloped their faces. Kaiden's grandfather pulled his daughter close as they strode toward us. He leaned in to kiss the side of her temple.

This was good. It had to be.

I didn't wait for them to reach us. I threaded through people's outstretched legs to get to them.

"Is he …?" My eyes frantically scanned their faces.

"Yes, he's got a lot of healing ahead of him. But the doctor gave Kaiden a good prognosis." Mrs. Carter's eyes glimmered with unshed tears.

"He's going to be okay?" I repeated. Her words not yet settling in my head.

A soft sob escaped her mouth as she pulled me into a snug embrace. "Yes, he is going to be okay."

"But there was so much blood?" I said when she released me.

"He hit his head hard enough to be unconscious for a bit. But they did the CT scan and cleared him of any brain damage. The doctor said he must have a guardian angel because his outcome could've been so much worse." A sheen covered her face, and I wondered if she was thinking of her belated husband.

I smiled at her and her parents. Lifting a hand, I rubbed the back of my neck and the grit of pressure on my teeth lessened.

Mrs. Carter continued, "Besides the concussion, he has

multiple broken ribs, a fractured hip, and a broken arm. His shoulder was dislocated, but they set it. A large cut on his head was most likely the cause for all the blood. Tomorrow, he will have surgery for the fracture. So he isn't in the clear yet and will be in a great deal of pain."

"Surgery? My God, poor Kaiden." I sighed, hugging my arm to my chest.

Tonight, Chad escaped charges for murder, but what about the next time? Would there be a next time? What would be the repercussions of his actions? When Chad sobered up, would he reflect on how bad this could have been?

Sometime later, we were permitted to see Kaiden. Mr. B and Mom waited in the waiting room while Kaiden's family, Finn, and I went to visit him.

When we entered the room, my hand shot to my mouth, muffling my cry. Kaiden lay in his hospital bed with his eyes closed. His face was turned to the side resting on his pillow. His head had been partly shaved, revealing a grisly five-inch line of stitches, and his face was swollen with bruises and cuts. He wore a cast on his left arm.

Finn wedged his hand in mine. His constant companionship and assurance had gotten me through this night this far.

Mrs. Carter leaned over her son and tenderly kissed his cheek.

"We are all here, Kaiden," she said softly.

He stirred and looked up at her. "Mom?"

"Yes, baby, it's me. Grandma, Grandpa, Jewel, and Finn are here also."

He turned, his eyes contemplating who stood at the bottom of his hospital bed. His eyes flicker from one face to another before resting on me.

"Beauty, I missed you." His handsome face broke into a winning smile.

A weightlessness captured my inner being, and I grinned. Maybe it was the good drugs pumping through his IV. I didn't know. But in his display of the Kaiden we knew and loved, tension and worries fled from the room.

Later, I sat in the back of Kaiden's grandparents' Town Car as we left the hospital. My finger traced the raindrops beating against my window. I thought back over the evening. A night that had been a magical fairy tale until the accident. In a blink of an eye, our lives could have been altered. But a miracle had occurred and mercy was given.

# CHAPTER THIRTY-ONE

*Jewel*

S ummer had come and gone, and Kaiden was almost fully recovered from the accident and his surgery. Finn and I spent most of the summer at Kaiden's house, finding ways to entertain him and keep his spirits high. We spent days on end spread out in the family room watching back-to-back TV series and playing cards, resulting in me becoming a card shark.

The Carters sued Chad, and it appeared the Carters would win the case. Chad learned nothing from his stunt of drinking and driving and almost taking a life. A few weeks ago, he was arrested for drug trafficking and was currently facing another court date.

Today, Finn, Kaiden, and I planned to visit Amy's grave for the first time and place some flowers. From my room, I heard Kaiden speaking to my family downstairs. In my closet inside a shoe box, I retrieved the sealed envelope with the letter from Amy. Folding it, I shoved it into the back pocket of my shorts.

Their laughter drifted from below, and a smile pulled at me. I loved my life. Every day, I woke up looking forward to what the day held in store.

Later, we walked through the cemetery to find her grave. The sight of her headstone halted a breath in each of us. Finn bent and laid a single yellow rose along the edge of the stone. Kaiden and I added our bouquet of wildflowers.

Stepping back, I reflected on the girl who'd been part of the turning point in my life. Though our friendship had been cut short, she permeated a void in me in a mere few months.

"I wanted to share something with you guys," I said, turning to them.

"Okay?" they said

"Remember I told you she left a letter? I wasn't able to open it when Mrs. Kent gave it to me, and I forgot about it until the other day when Finn suggested coming here. I thought it would be fitting to read it here today with you guys."

"I often wonder why she never left me one," Finn said, never lifting his eyes from her grave. "I'd thought maybe in the chaos of that day, a letter to me might have gotten misplaced. Maybe I would've found some kind of closure if she had. When you told me she left you one, I couldn't help but feel envious."

My heart ached for him. "I'm sorry, Finn. I don't think we will ever totally understand everything about Amy. I wish this letter were for you, but maybe you will find something in it that will help you move on."

"Maybe."

Taking the letter from my pocket, I handed it to Kaiden.

"Will you read it?"

"Sure," he said. He opened the envelope and unfolded the paper. He briefly gazed over it, and his eyes widened. "It's for all of us."

"What?" Finn and I said together.

Kaiden gazed back at the letter and began to read:

*To my friends,*

*If you're reading this, then my life is over. I know you will try but don't blame yourselves. These past few months were the best months of my life. Try not to reflect on what you all could've done to save me. I've been lost for far too long.*

*Don't dwell on the past or my death. I'll be looking down on graduation day and prom night. I'll see you dolled up and looking fine. Finn, you would've been the most handsome prom date of them all.*

*In your memories, my spirit will live on. In the star that shines extra bright at night, you will find me. The rain will be my kiss, and the warmth of the sun, my embrace.*

*Don't be sad for me. Go on and live. Enjoy your lives. Because now ... I'm free.*

*All my love,*

*Amy*

Sweet silent tears trickled down my cheeks. Kaiden cleared his throat and wiped at the corner of his eyes before folding the letter and handing it back to me.

Finn removed his glasses and wiped his eyes with the

hem of his tank top.

"Here, Finn, you keep this."

"What? Are you sure?"

"Yes. She would've wanted you to have the letter. Besides when I need to hear her words, I'll know where to find it." I smiled.

He reached for the letter, and caressing the paper, he moved it to his lips before tucking the letter in his shorts pocket.

"She was a hell of a girl, wasn't she?" he beamed as we turned to walk back to my car.

"She had to be, to be love struck by the likes of you." Kaiden clapped him on the back.

Finn smirked. "So what does that say for Jewel? Because I told you what I thought of your type from day one."

Kaiden laughed. "But I did prove you wrong, didn't I?"

"I guess maybe you did." Finn joined in his laughter.

"Well, I think you're both a little crazy. But the kind of crazy I like." I slipped an arm around each of their waists.

"What's the saying again? A rose between two thorns or something?" Kaiden chuckled as we reached the car.

"The two thorns I'm now stuck with since you both decided to follow me to Calgary," I jested.

"Kaiden is to blame for that, and there was no way I was being left behind," Finn added as he ducked into the back seat.

I peeked over the roof of my car at Kaiden and smiled. We were told the healer of an aching heart was time because we couldn't change the past. But the future was ours for the making. Adventure awaited around the next corner. Together, we were ready to take on the world.

# Acknowledgments

I want to give a special thank you to Caroline Kraiser for guiding me back in the direction I originally wanted to take my manuscript but was too scared to go. Your words of wisdom helped me shine a light on the truth I wanted to tell.

I also wanted to thank Jenny Sims for her kindness and guidance throughout this whole experience. You have helped me more than you will ever know.

# ABOUT THE AUTHOR

Jane lives life to the full because she doesn't want to wake up twenty years from now regretting all the things she didn't do. She's an avid traveler who also loves throwing elaborate dinner parties where she wows her guests with gourmet meals. Jane has a passion for writing, interior design, history, movies, board games, and fitness. In her quest for an exciting life, however, she now draws the line at zip-lining, which she experienced in Costa Rica. Never again!

Jane comes from a family of six sisters and lived in a Tennessee plantation house for several years while growing up. She now lives in Western Canada but dreams of owning a vacation home in South Carolina. She lives with her husband (her high school sweetheart), two teenagers, and two dogs. When she grows up, she'd like to be her brilliant sixteen-year-old daughter (minus the mood swings)

www.authorjanecbrady.com

# PREVIEW OF
# ECHOES IN THE STREETS

## PROLOGUE

**Remi**

*15 Years Prior*

My mother's blood-curdling screams echoed through our cramped two-bedroom bungalow. I remember my sweaty bare feet sticking to the 1970 linoleum flooring as I crept down the hallway, tugging my frayed fleece baby blanket behind me. Drawing closer to the living room, I lifted the blanket with knotted hands, shielding my face. Daddy was drunk again. He always hurt her when he had too many drinks at the pub.

"Ted stop! Calm down," Mom cried.

I peeked around the corner of the archway as she

scrambled around the back of the couch, trying to avoid his grasp. A nasty welt highlighted the side of her face, and her nose gushed with fresh crimson blood. Fear swelled in the back of my throat as tears blinded my vision.

Daddy's long legs moved fast. They always did, but my mom had spent her life dodging his grasp, and she scurried around the other side.

My five-year-old legs shook, and a soft muffled whimper fell from me, "Mommy?"

"Go, Remi! Please go." She didn't dare take her eyes off Daddy.

I wanted to help her. I needed to help because he always hurt her bad. He was the monster in the closet; the man staring in my window. Daddy was the bogeyman. I was too little to help and getting in the middle only made him angrier and caused her to fight harder.

"I'm going to kill you!" he yelled. His face a dark shade of purple and his eyes bulged as he dashed around the back of the couch. She once again evaded his grip and scrambled to the other side of the room.

"Mommy," I called again.

"Baby, please, run. Go!" Her dark eyes dampened as she pleaded with me.

He lunged at her and captured her arm with his massive hand, she squealed and pounded him with her fist. I cringed as my eyes moved from my mother's face to the hand holding her prisoner. Daddy's hands weren't gentle. They were mean hands and afflicted pain whenever they came near.

Shivers penetrated my body as deep rumbling laughter came from way down in his chest. The veins and cords of his neck distended as his hold compressed her throat.

"Have I taught you nothing, Sara? I will always be faster than you." With a single hand, he pinned her against the freshly painted walls.

Mom and I had gone to the local Home Depot and purchased the paint. It had been the perfect day. On the way home, we stopped for ice cream. She laughed and kissed me as we sat on the park bench licking our sweet sugary goodness. Later, as I sat coloring, she had hung from a ladder rolling the sage green paint on the walls, her beautiful voice belting out her favorite country tunes playing in the background.

Dragged away from my memory, I watched as his grip squeezed her delicate neck, and he raised her higher and higher. Her legs dangled, and one of her brown ballerina flats hit the ground, drawing my eyes to the discarded shoe for a split second. The slapping of flesh against flesh returned my attention back to my parents. My mother slapped her hands at his face and arms, trying to free herself. Her eyes protruded, and her face turned a purplish-gray. My dad's face filled with a grimace as he squeezed tighter. Her body wiggled and thrashed as she struggled for life.

She couldn't breathe. She didn't look right.

"Daddy! Stop. You're hurting her," I screamed.

He didn't pay me any mind. It was as if I didn't exist in his blackout rage.

My mom clawed at the fingers restricting her airflow.

"Stop …" I charged at him, beating at his legs with my fist. "Let her go. She can't breathe."

He kicked out his leg and sent me flying, my head cracking on the corner of the coffee table. A hot liquid leaked between my legs, soaking my favorite Disney princess pajamas. The smell of pee filled the air.

I shifted my eyes back to my parents. I'll never forget watching the light leave my mother's eyes and her hands stop fighting. Her body went limp, and my father discarded her body without even a blink.

He turned his glassy eyes on me and the look in his eyes choked me with fear. I dashed to my feet and ran down the hall.

"I'll find you, Remi." His booming voice carried through the house. The clicking of his cowboy boots resonated as they left the carpet of the living room and advanced down the hallway.

I was screaming at him in my mind. *No, no, no, Daddy. Stop.*

The breeze of his fingers as he reached for the back of my pajama shirt pushed my legs faster.

*Where can I go? How can I get out of here?* The hallway was ending, and my eyes locked on the back door. The door was tricky to open and often jammed from the settling of the house.

I caught sight of the doggie door. My best friend had been a German Shepard by the name of Buck, but my dad had shot him when he tried to defend my mother. I leaped through the doggie door and tumbled onto the back deck.

My dad fumbled with the door handle. I didn't wait for him to open it. I found my legs and ran down the rickety stairs. My feet hit the plush grass from the few days of recent rain.

I ran to the gate leading out onto the street. Dad's feet trudged across the deck, and I swallowed hard.

His feet landed with a heavy thud on the grass.

"There you are. You always were quick on your feet, but

Daddy will get you now. You can't get away."

I pulled on the gate. It wouldn't budge. I noticed the padlock Dad had secured to the latch days prior. My eyes darted around, trying to find a way out. It was then I recalled the missing board in the fence.

I bolted for the small opening. I was too big. My mind was racing and begging for mercy *I must fit. Please no, Daddy. Don't hurt me.*

I wiggled and fought to squirm through the fence. Turning my head sideways, the fence released me as his hand grabbed me. I squealed as his fingers caught the neck of my pjs and his nails tore at my flesh, I wrestled myself out of my shirt. I was free. Our eyes met, and the loathing of the demon-possessed man in the dark seared into my memory.

I charged across the lawn, his curses trailing behind me. The glow of the streetlights lit my path, concrete scratching my feet as I ran. My legs were heavy with exhaustion, my chest threatening to explode.

I tossed my head left and right, desperately searching for help. The house of the nice old man who often greeted my mom and me when we were out for walks came into view. I pushed open his front gate and pounded up his front steps.

"Mr. Calder!" I wailed, beating on his front door, casting a glance over my shoulder out into the street.

He was coming!

Panic consumed me and my terror heightened, "Mr. Calder!" I shrieked, wiggling the handle.

The porch light flicked on and someone within fumbled to unlock the door.

"Hurry, please hurry."

The door flew open as the gate rattled.

He was at the gate.

"Young Remi what—" Mr. Calder's voice broke as he glimpsed my dad in his lunatic state. He shoved me inside, slamming the door behind him. Locking the deadbolt, he slid the chain across. The thundering of my dad's footsteps on the porch sent me clinging to Mr. Calder's legs.

"He killed Mommy. He killed her," I sobbed.

The hammering of Dad's fist on the door vibrated the window panes.

Mr. Calder dialed 911. I watched from the front windows of his house as the lights of the police cars and ambulance lit up our neighborhood. My dad was long gone before they arrived. People in uniforms surrounded me, asking me questions I couldn't answer. Mr. Calder had wrapped a blanket around my naked torso, but it didn't relieve the quiver coursing through my body.

A lady with dark hair tied in a knot at the nape of her neck came for me. She put me in her car and took me away.

This began the first of five foster homes that would continue to affect my life in a negative way.

My dad's actions resulted in a manhunt which lasted for weeks before he was apprehended and sentenced to life in prison.

61150721R00158

Made in the USA
Middletown, DE
08 January 2018